D0603411

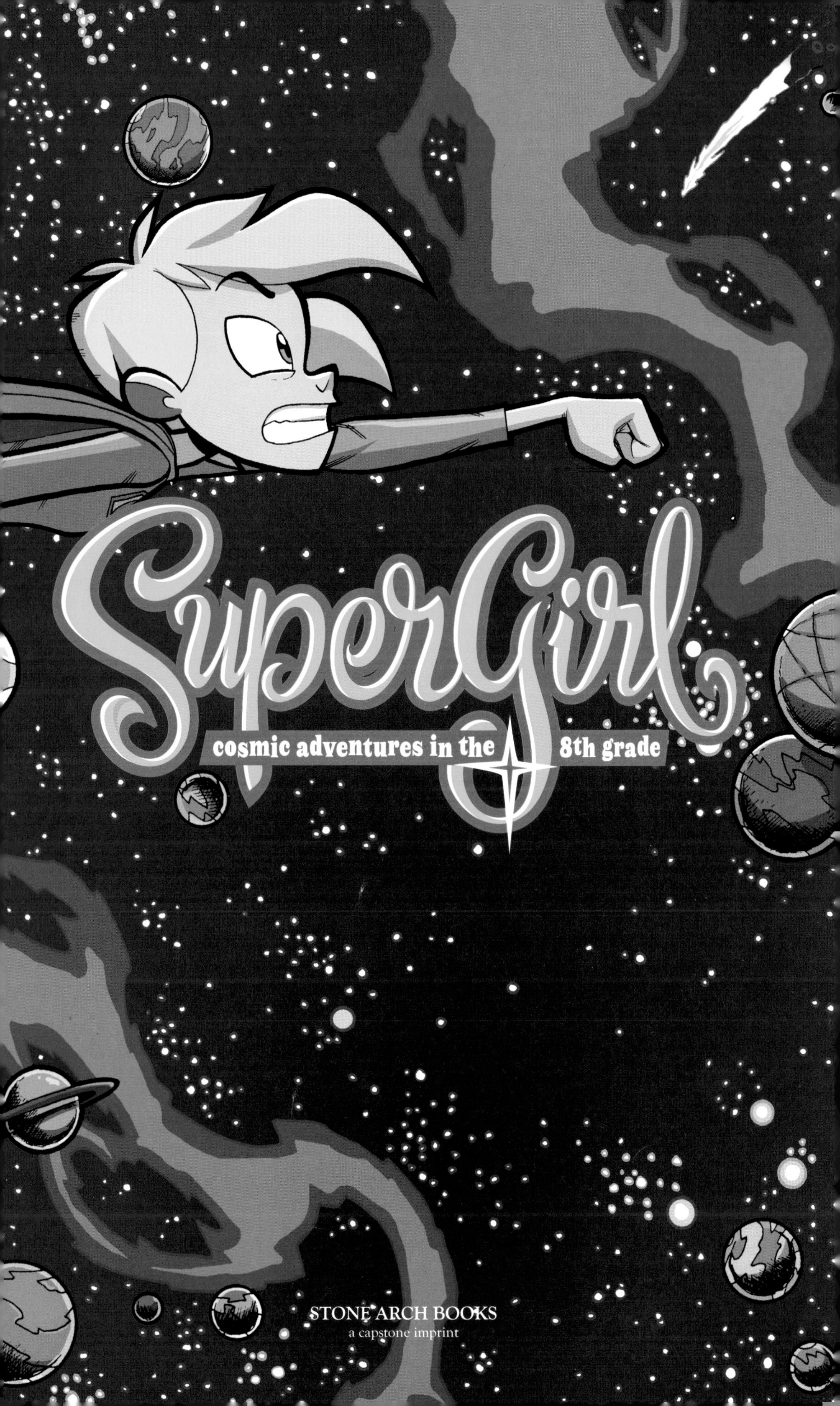
SuperGirl
cosmic adventures in the 8th grade

STONE ARCH BOOKS
a capstone imprint

STONE ARCH BOOKS™
Published in 2013
A Capstone Imprint
1710 Roe Crest Drive
North Mankato, MN 56003
www.capstonepub.com

Originally published by DC Comics in the U.S. in single magazine form as Supergirl: Cosmic Adventures in the 8th Grade #5.

Cataloging-in-Publication Data is available at the Library of Congress website:
ISBN: 978-1-4342-6045-1 (library binding)

Summary: It's graduation day, and things couldn't be more complicated! The whole gang is here, and the cosmic craziness is about to get way out of hand!

STONE ARCH BOOKS
Ashley C. Andersen Zantop Publisher
Michael Dahl Editorial Director
Donald Lemke Editor
Heather Kindseth Creative Director
Brann Garvey Designer
Kathy McColley Production Specialist

DC COMICS
Jann Jones & Elisabeth V. Gehrlein Original U.S. Editors
Adam Schlagman U.S. Associate Editor
Simona Martore U.S. Assistant Editor

DC Comics
1700 Broadway, New York, NY 10019
A Warner Bros. Entertainment Company

Printed in China by Nordica.
0413/CA21300442
032013 007226NORDF13

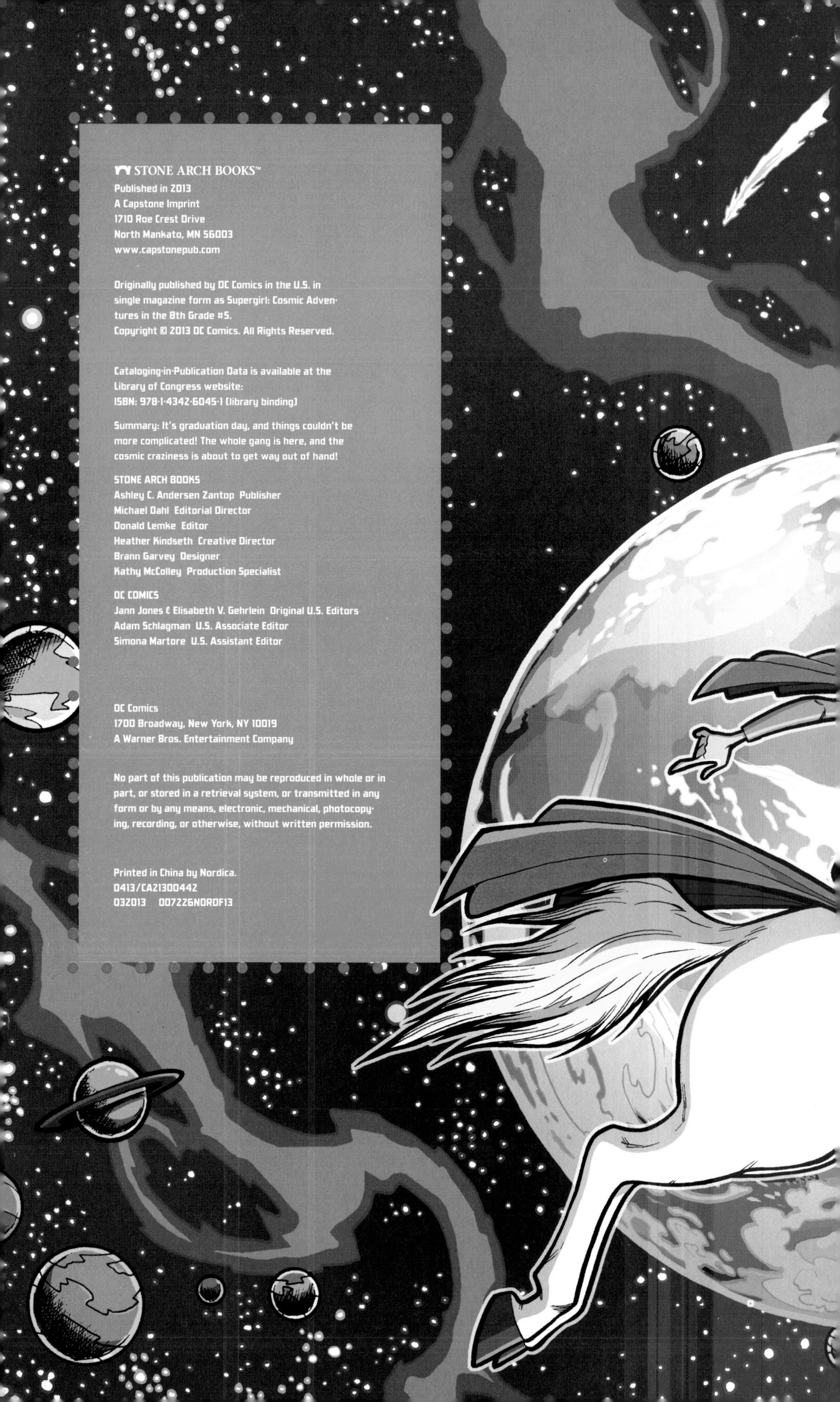

SuperGirl
cosmic adventures in the 8th grade

EVIL IN A SKIRT!

LANDRY Q. WALKER
WRITER

ERIC JONES
ARTIST

JOEY MASON
COLORIST

PAT BROSSEAU
TRAVIS LANHAM
SAL CIPRIANO
LETTERERS

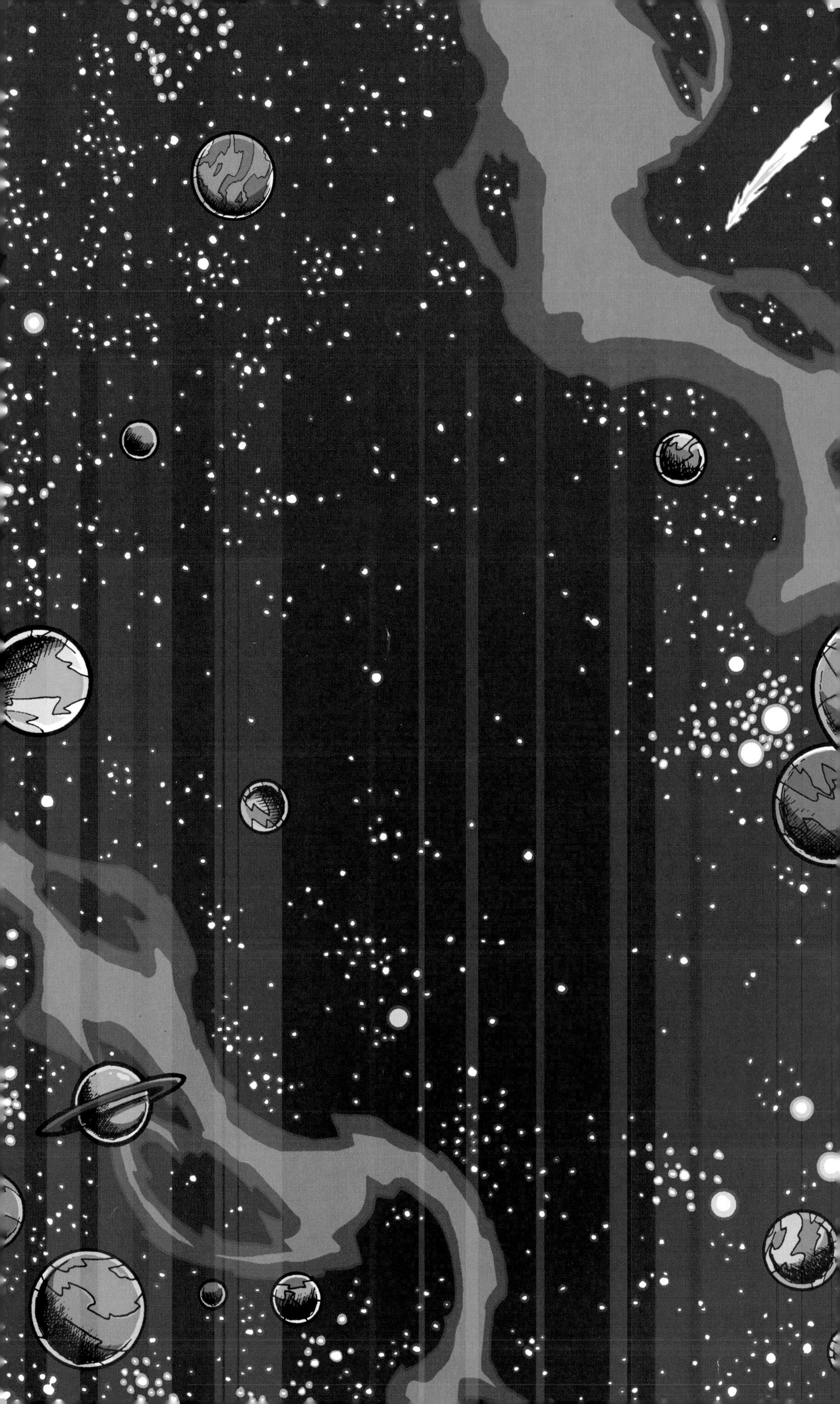

GRADUATION DAY PART 1

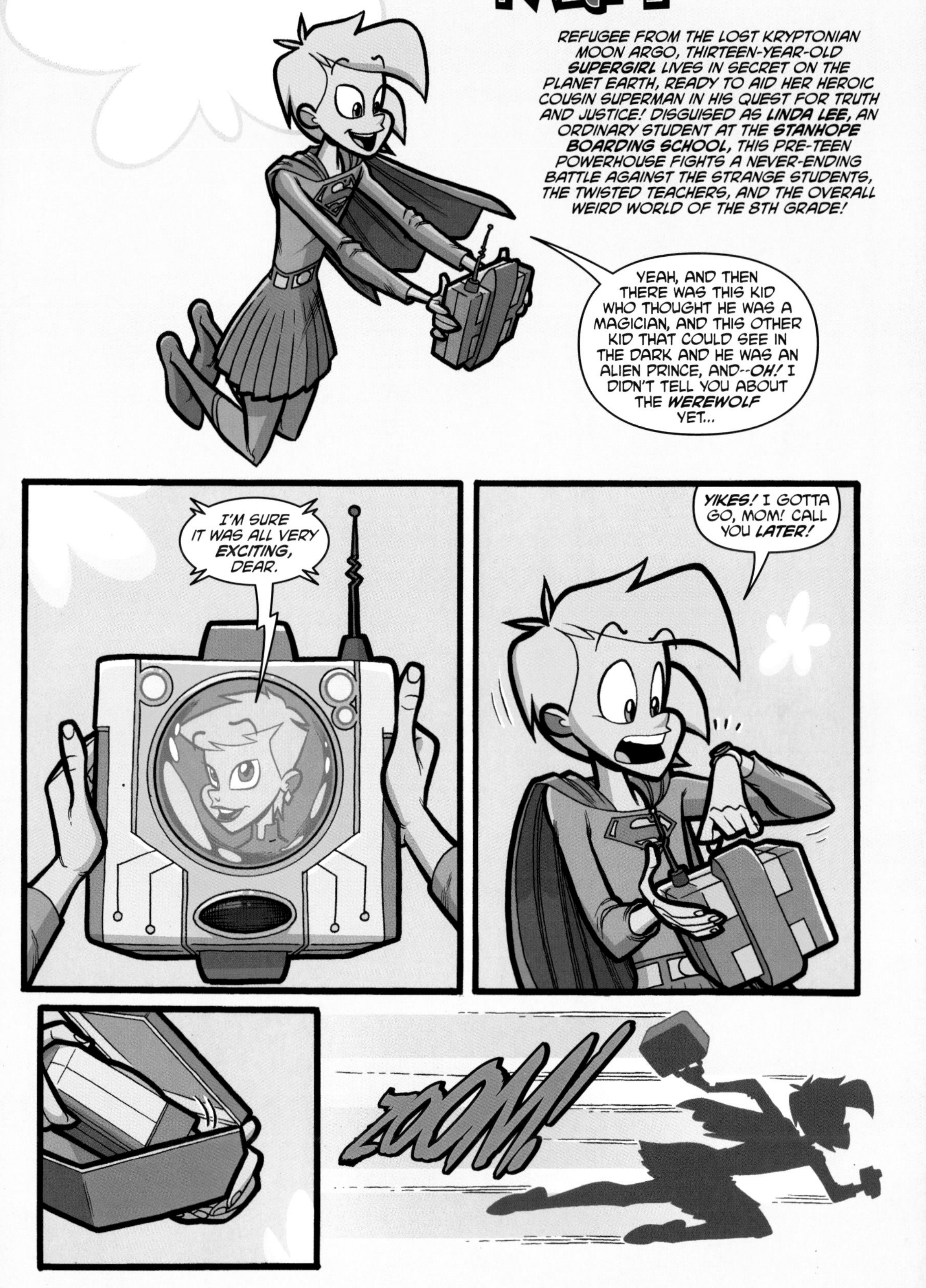
REFUGEE FROM THE LOST KRYPTONIAN MOON ARGO, THIRTEEN-YEAR-OLD **SUPERGIRL** LIVES IN SECRET ON THE PLANET EARTH, READY TO AID HER HEROIC COUSIN SUPERMAN IN HIS QUEST FOR TRUTH AND JUSTICE! DISGUISED AS **LINDA LEE**, AN ORDINARY STUDENT AT THE **STANHOPE BOARDING SCHOOL**, THIS PRE-TEEN POWERHOUSE FIGHTS A NEVER-ENDING BATTLE AGAINST THE STRANGE STUDENTS, THE TWISTED TEACHERS, AND THE OVERALL WEIRD WORLD OF THE 8TH GRADE!
YEAH, AND THEN THERE WAS THIS KID WHO THOUGHT HE WAS A MAGICIAN, AND THIS OTHER KID THAT COULD SEE IN THE DARK AND HE WAS AN ALIEN PRINCE, AND--*OH!* I DIDN'T TELL YOU ABOUT THE ***WEREWOLF*** YET...
I'M SURE IT WAS ALL VERY *EXCITING*, DEAR.
YIKES! I GOTTA GO, MOM! CALL YOU ***LATER!***
ZOOM!

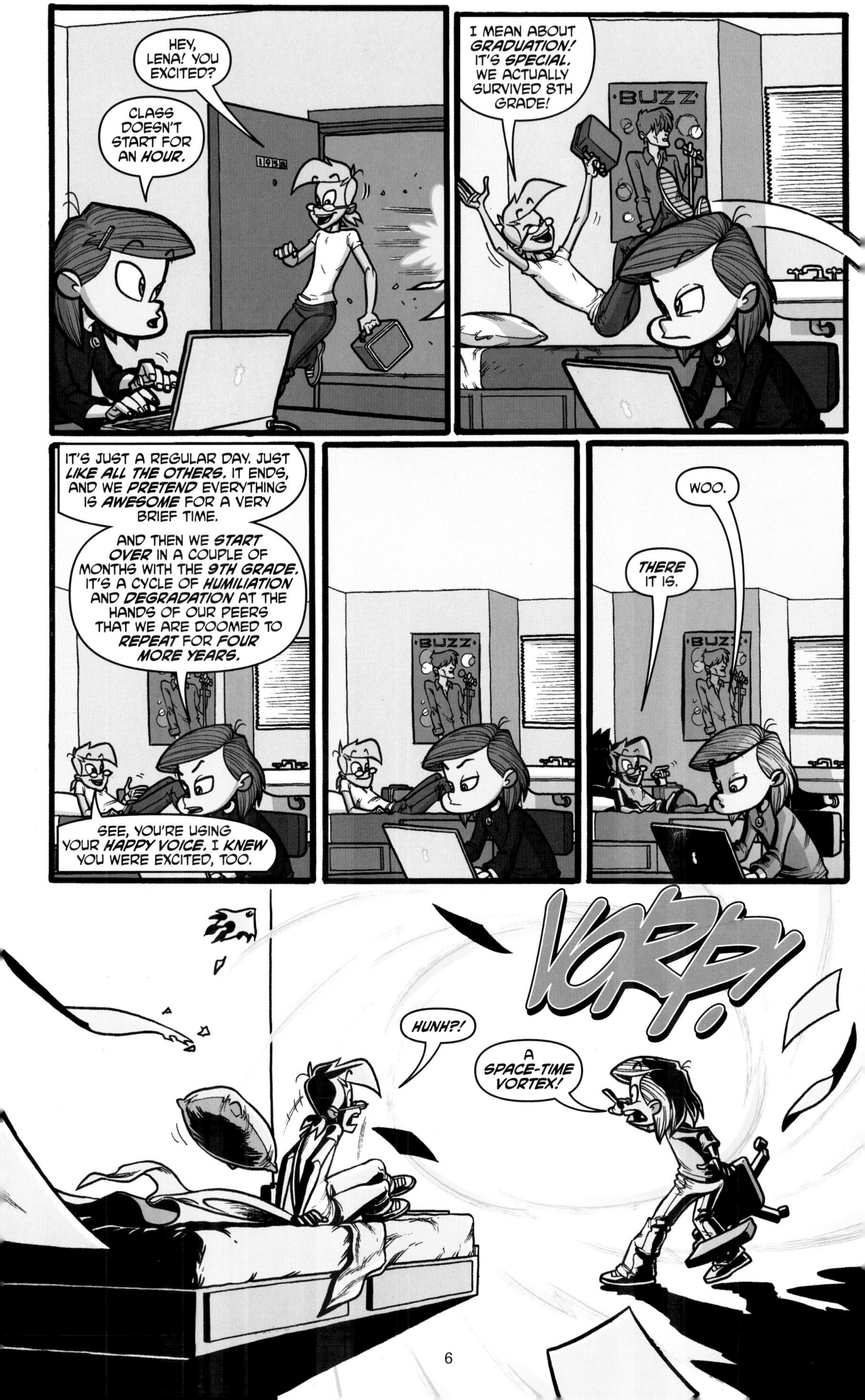
HEY, LENA! YOU EXCITED?
CLASS DOESN'T START FOR AN HOUR.
I MEAN ABOUT GRADUATION! IT'S SPECIAL. WE ACTUALLY SURVIVED 8TH GRADE!
BUZZ
IT'S JUST A REGULAR DAY. JUST LIKE ALL THE OTHERS. IT ENDS, AND WE PRETEND EVERYTHING IS AWESOME FOR A VERY BRIEF TIME.
AND THEN WE START OVER IN A COUPLE OF MONTHS WITH THE 9TH GRADE. IT'S A CYCLE OF HUMILIATION AND DEGRADATION AT THE HANDS OF OUR PEERS THAT WE ARE DOOMED TO REPEAT FOR FOUR MORE YEARS.
SEE, YOU'RE USING YOUR HAPPY VOICE. I KNEW YOU WERE EXCITED, TOO.
BUZZ
WOO.
THERE IT IS.
VORP!
HUNH?!
A SPACE-TIME VORTEX!

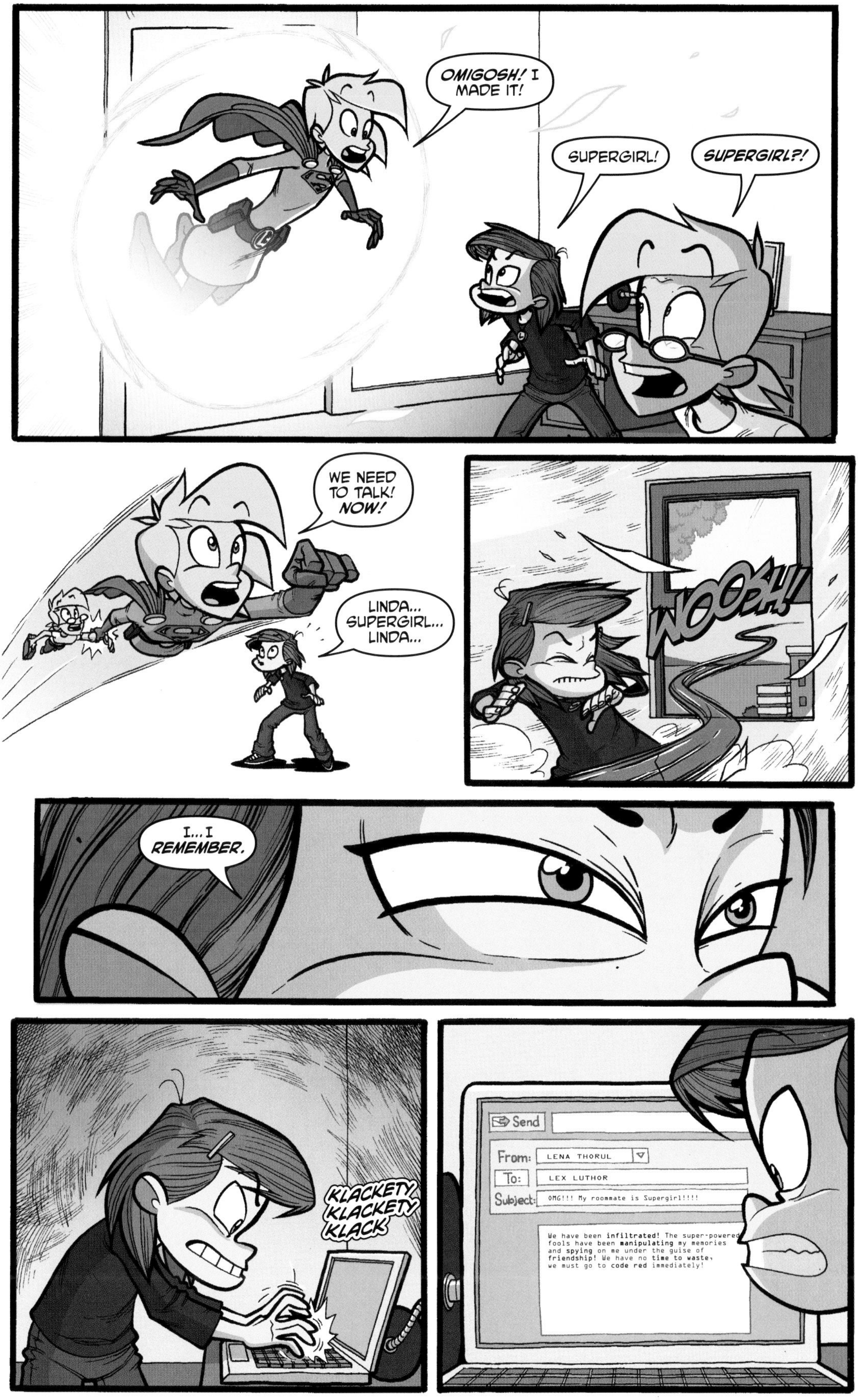
OMIGOSH! I MADE IT!
SUPERGIRL!
SUPERGIRL?!
WE NEED TO TALK! NOW!
LINDA... SUPERGIRL... LINDA...
WOOSH!
I... I REMEMBER.
KLACKETY KLACKETY KLACK
Send
From: LENA THORUL
To: LEX LUTHOR
Subject: OMG!!! My roommate is Supergirl!!!!
We have been infiltrated! The super-powered fools have been manipulating my memories and spying on me under the guise of friendship! We have no time to waste, we must go to code red immediately!

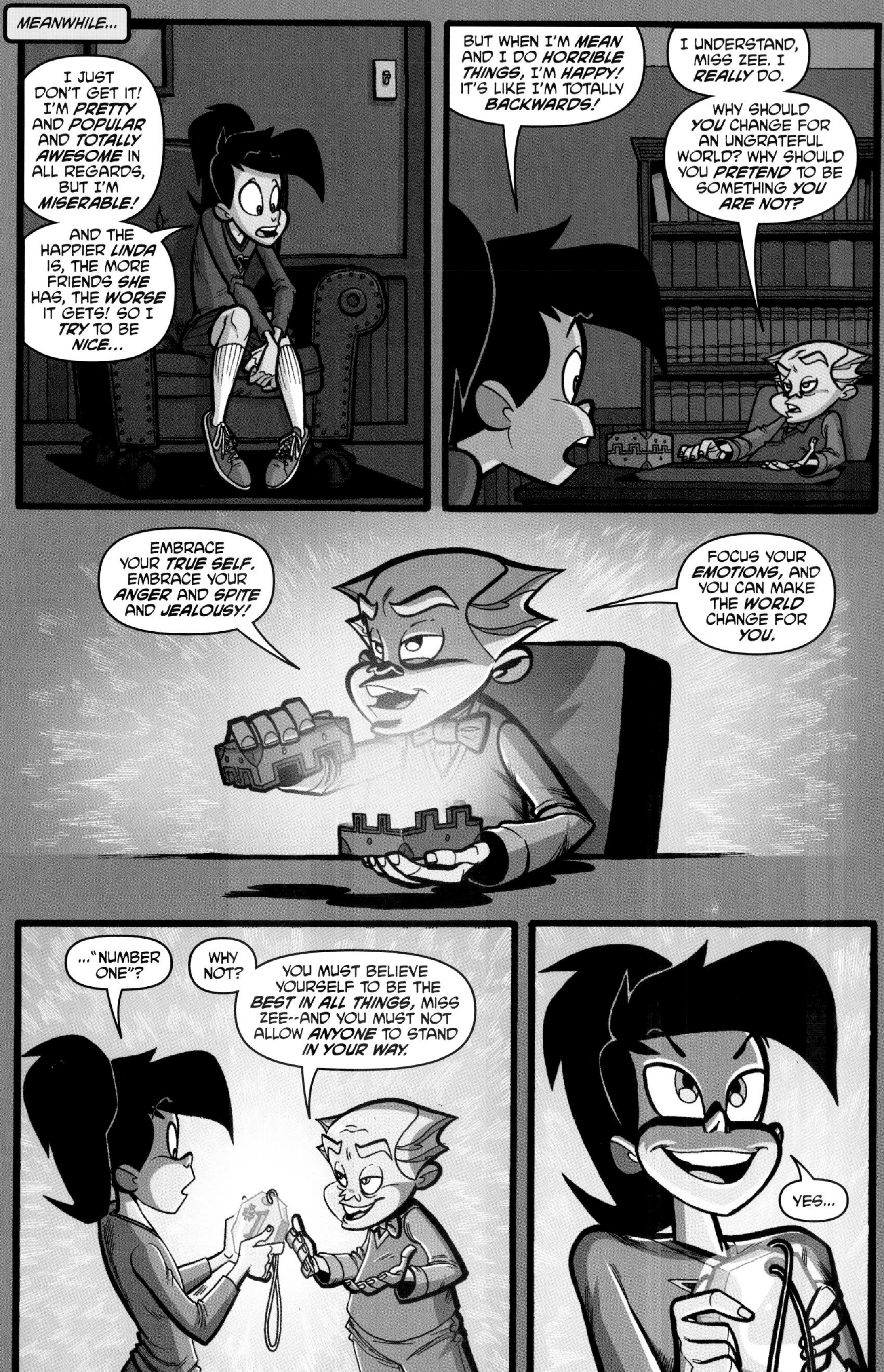
MEANWHILE...
I JUST DON'T GET IT! I'M PRETTY AND POPULAR AND TOTALLY AWESOME IN ALL REGARDS, BUT I'M MISERABLE!
AND THE HAPPIER LINDA IS, THE MORE FRIENDS SHE HAS, THE WORSE IT GETS! SO I TRY TO BE NICE...
BUT WHEN I'M MEAN AND I DO HORRIBLE THINGS, I'M HAPPY! IT'S LIKE I'M TOTALLY BACKWARDS!
I UNDERSTAND, MISS ZEE. I REALLY DO.
WHY SHOULD YOU CHANGE FOR AN UNGRATEFUL WORLD? WHY SHOULD YOU PRETEND TO BE SOMETHING YOU ARE NOT?
EMBRACE YOUR TRUE SELF. EMBRACE YOUR ANGER AND SPITE AND JEALOUSY!
FOCUS YOUR EMOTIONS, AND YOU CAN MAKE THE WORLD CHANGE FOR YOU.
..."NUMBER ONE"?
WHY NOT?
YOU MUST BELIEVE YOURSELF TO BE THE BEST IN ALL THINGS, MISS ZEE--AND YOU MUST NOT ALLOW ANYONE TO STAND IN YOUR WAY.
YES...

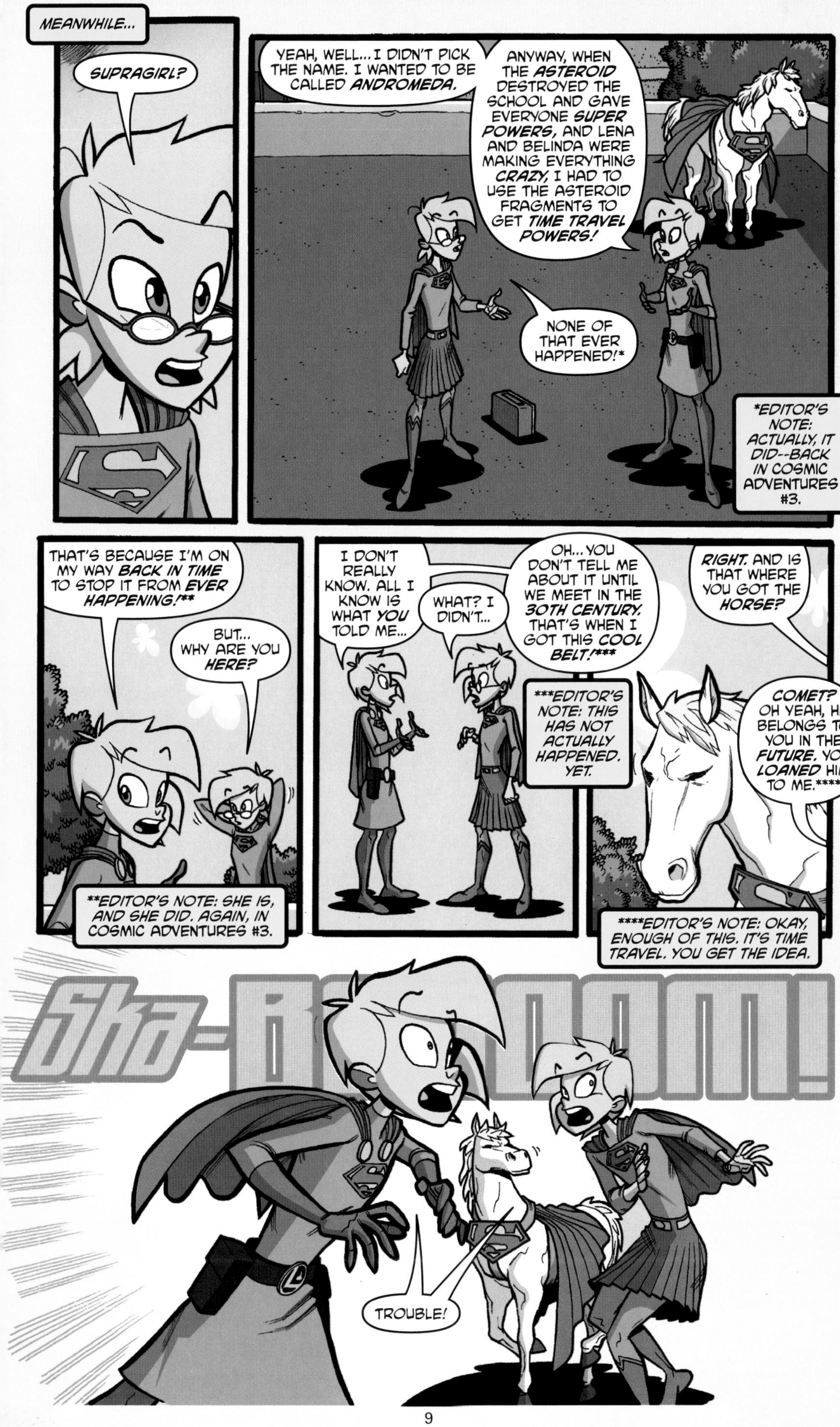

MEANWHILE...
SUPRAGIRL?
YEAH, WELL... I DIDN'T PICK THE NAME. I WANTED TO BE CALLED ANDROMEDA.
ANYWAY, WHEN THE ASTEROID DESTROYED THE SCHOOL AND GAVE EVERYONE SUPER POWERS, AND LENA AND BELINDA WERE MAKING EVERYTHING CRAZY, I HAD TO USE THE ASTEROID FRAGMENTS TO GET TIME TRAVEL POWERS!
NONE OF THAT EVER HAPPENED!*
*EDITOR'S NOTE: ACTUALLY, IT DID--BACK IN COSMIC ADVENTURES #3.
THAT'S BECAUSE I'M ON MY WAY BACK IN TIME TO STOP IT FROM EVER HAPPENING!**
BUT... WHY ARE YOU HERE?
**EDITOR'S NOTE: SHE IS, AND SHE DID. AGAIN, IN COSMIC ADVENTURES #3.
I DON'T REALLY KNOW. ALL I KNOW IS WHAT YOU TOLD ME...
WHAT? I DIDN'T...
OH... YOU DON'T TELL ME ABOUT IT UNTIL WE MEET IN THE 30TH CENTURY. THAT'S WHEN I GOT THIS COOL BELT!***
***EDITOR'S NOTE: THIS HAS NOT ACTUALLY HAPPENED. YET.
RIGHT. AND IS THAT WHERE YOU GOT THE HORSE?
COMET? OH YEAH, HE BELONGS TO YOU IN THE FUTURE. YOU LOANED HIM TO ME.****
****EDITOR'S NOTE: OKAY, ENOUGH OF THIS. IT'S TIME TRAVEL. YOU GET THE IDEA.
SKA-BOOOM!
TROUBLE!

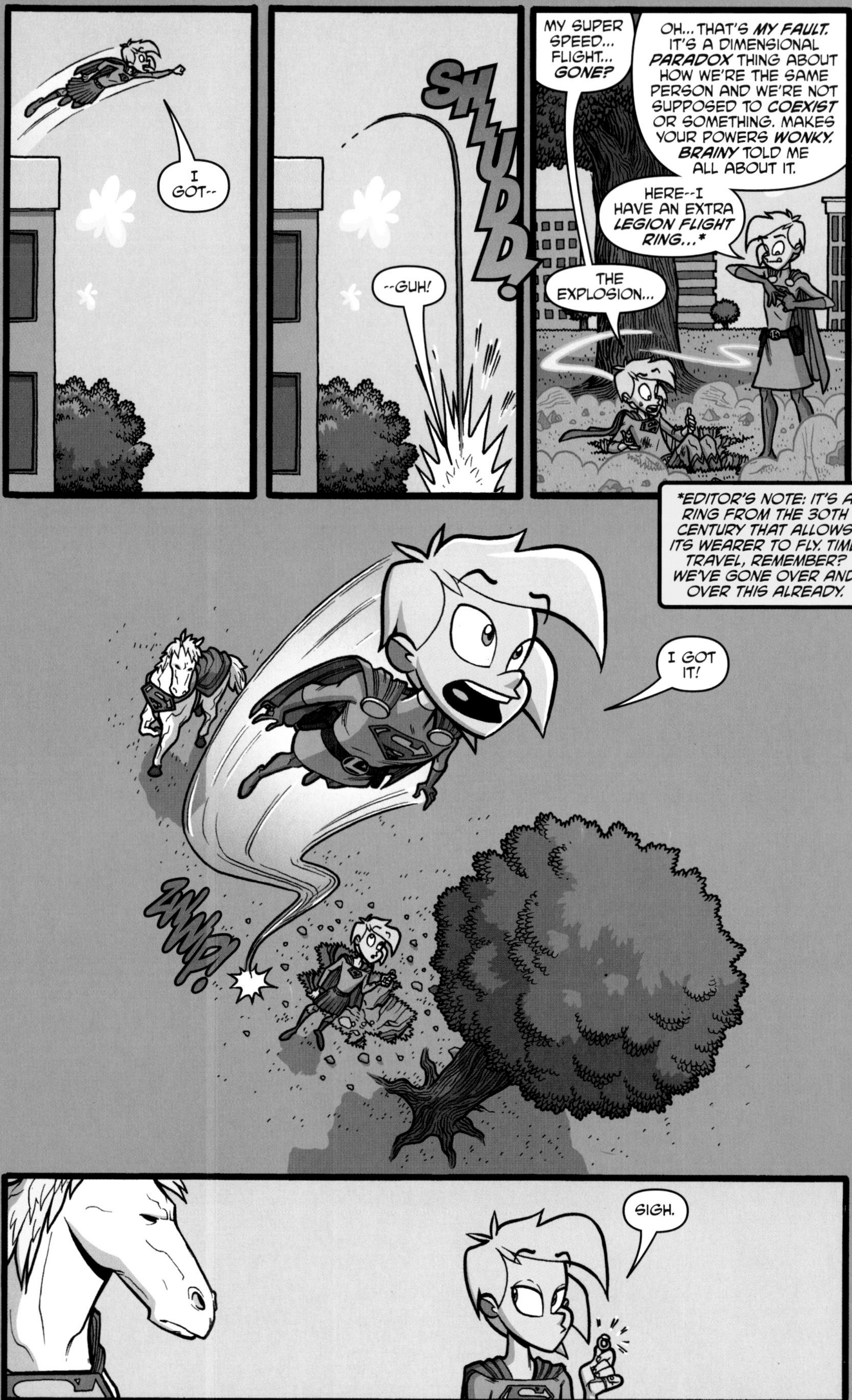
I GOT--
SHLUDD!
--GUH!
MY SUPER SPEED... FLIGHT... GONE?
OH... THAT'S MY FAULT. IT'S A DIMENSIONAL PARADOX THING ABOUT HOW WE'RE THE SAME PERSON AND WE'RE NOT SUPPOSED TO COEXIST OR SOMETHING. MAKES YOUR POWERS WONKY. BRAINY TOLD ME ALL ABOUT IT.
THE EXPLOSION...
HERE--I HAVE AN EXTRA LEGION FLIGHT RING...*
*EDITOR'S NOTE: IT'S A RING FROM THE 30TH CENTURY THAT ALLOWS ITS WEARER TO FLY. TIME TRAVEL, REMEMBER? WE'VE GONE OVER AND OVER THIS ALREADY.
I GOT IT!
ZWHUD!
SIGH.

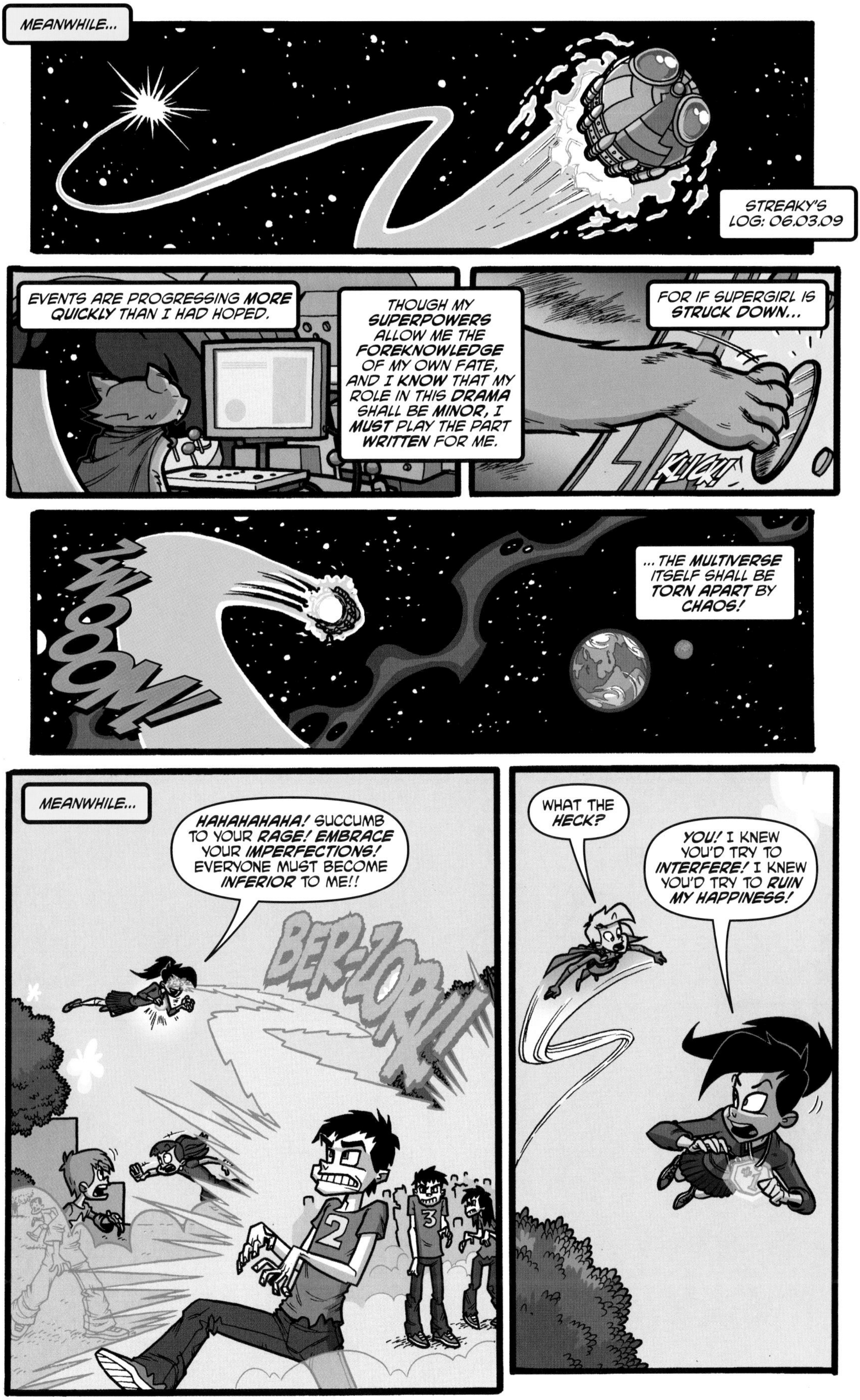
MEANWHILE...
STREAKY'S LOG: 06.03.09
EVENTS ARE PROGRESSING MORE QUICKLY THAN I HAD HOPED.
THOUGH MY SUPERPOWERS ALLOW ME THE FOREKNOWLEDGE OF MY OWN FATE, AND I KNOW THAT MY ROLE IN THIS DRAMA SHALL BE MINOR, I MUST PLAY THE PART WRITTEN FOR ME.
FOR IF SUPERGIRL IS STRUCK DOWN...
KLICK!
ZWOOOOM!
...THE MULTIVERSE ITSELF SHALL BE TORN APART BY CHAOS!
MEANWHILE...
HAHAHAHAHA! SUCCUMB TO YOUR RAGE! EMBRACE YOUR IMPERFECTIONS! EVERYONE MUST BECOME INFERIOR TO ME!!
BER-ZORK!
WHAT THE HECK?
YOU! I KNEW YOU'D TRY TO INTERFERE! I KNEW YOU'D TRY TO RUIN MY HAPPINESS!

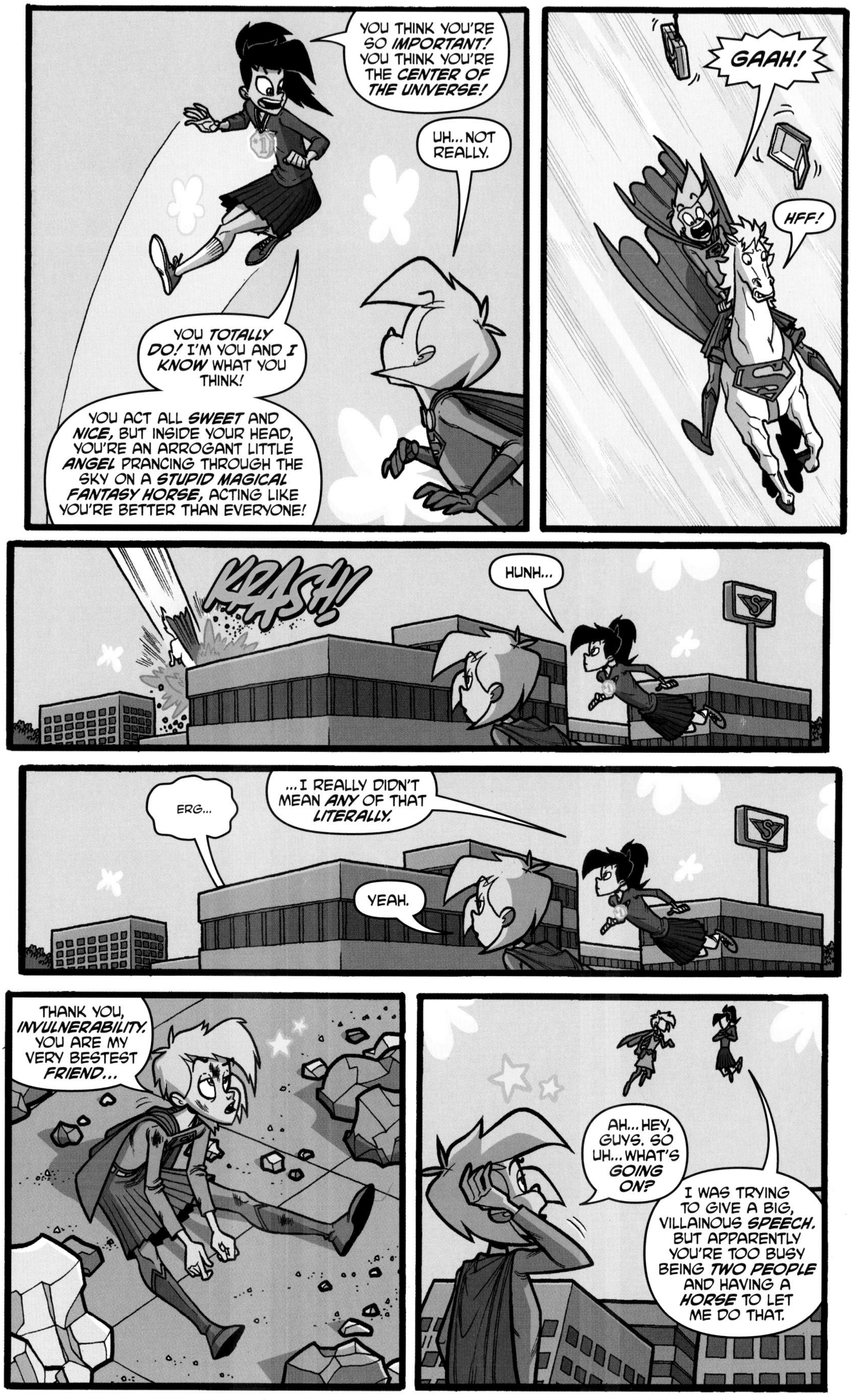
YOU THINK YOU'RE SO IMPORTANT! YOU THINK YOU'RE THE CENTER OF THE UNIVERSE!
UH... NOT REALLY.
YOU TOTALLY DO! I'M YOU AND I KNOW WHAT YOU THINK!
YOU ACT ALL SWEET AND NICE, BUT INSIDE YOUR HEAD, YOU'RE AN ARROGANT LITTLE ANGEL PRANCING THROUGH THE SKY ON A STUPID MAGICAL FANTASY HORSE, ACTING LIKE YOU'RE BETTER THAN EVERYONE!
GAAH!
HFF!
KRASH!
HUNH...
ERG...
...I REALLY DIDN'T MEAN ANY OF THAT LITERALLY.
YEAH.
THANK YOU, INVULNERABILITY. YOU ARE MY VERY BESTEST FRIEND...
AH... HEY, GUYS. SO UH... WHAT'S GOING ON?
I WAS TRYING TO GIVE A BIG, VILLAINOUS SPEECH. BUT APPARENTLY YOU'RE TOO BUSY BEING TWO PEOPLE AND HAVING A HORSE TO LET ME DO THAT.

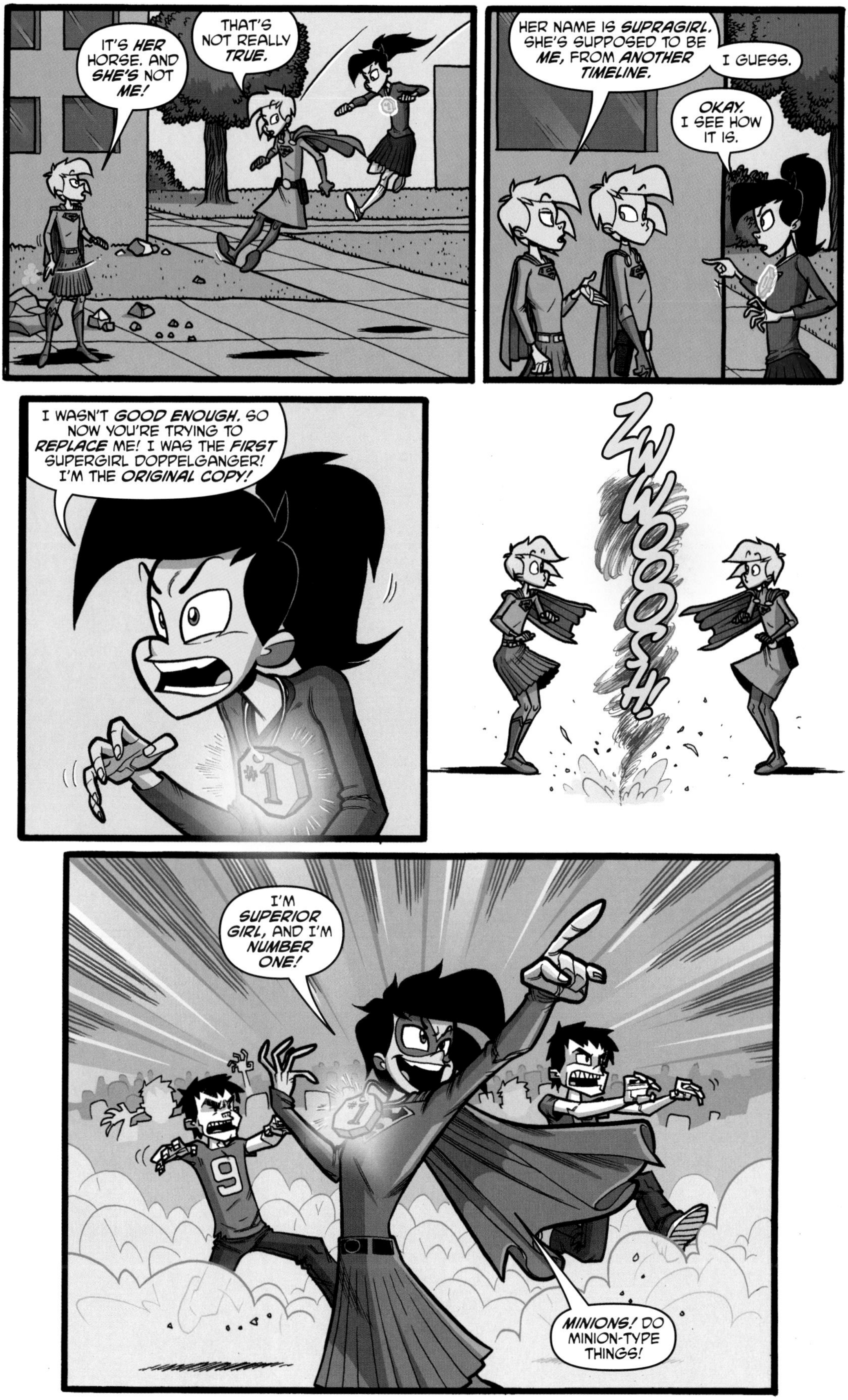
IT'S HER HORSE. AND SHE'S NOT ME!
THAT'S NOT REALLY TRUE.
HER NAME IS SUPRAGIRL. SHE'S SUPPOSED TO BE ME, FROM ANOTHER TIMELINE.
I GUESS.
OKAY. I SEE HOW IT IS.
I WASN'T GOOD ENOUGH. SO NOW YOU'RE TRYING TO REPLACE ME! I WAS THE FIRST SUPERGIRL DOPPELGANGER! I'M THE ORIGINAL COPY!
ZWOOOOSH!
I'M SUPERIOR GIRL, AND I'M NUMBER ONE!
MINIONS! DO MINION-TYPE THINGS!

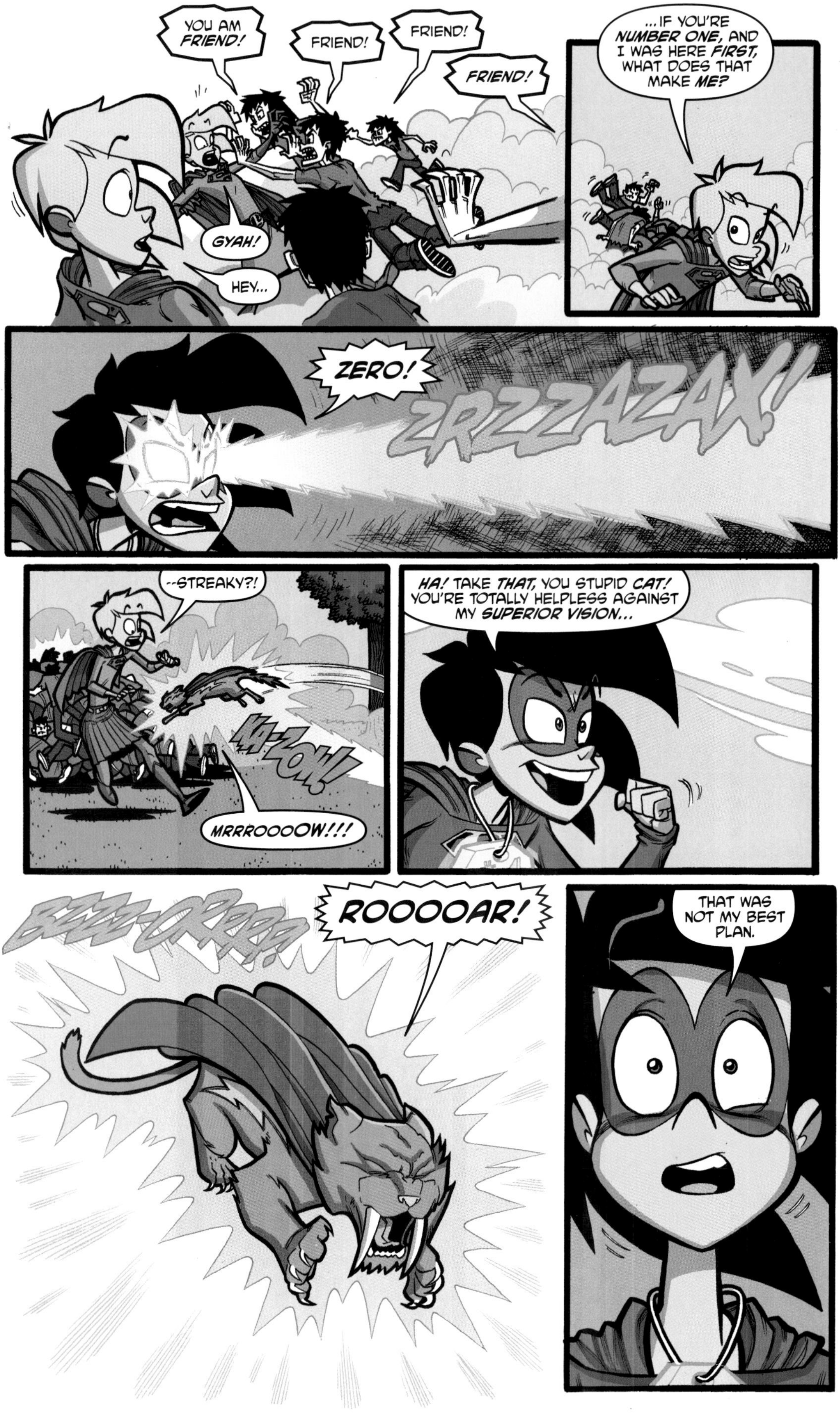
YOU AM FRIEND!
FRIEND!
FRIEND!
FRIEND!
GYAH!
HEY...
...IF YOU'RE NUMBER ONE, AND I WAS HERE FIRST, WHAT DOES THAT MAKE ME?
ZERO!
ZRZZZAZAX!
--STREAKY?!
KA-ZOW!
MRRROOOOW!!!
HA! TAKE THAT, YOU STUPID CAT! YOU'RE TOTALLY HELPLESS AGAINST MY SUPERIOR VISION...
BZZZ-ORRRP!
ROOOOAR!
THAT WAS NOT MY BEST PLAN.

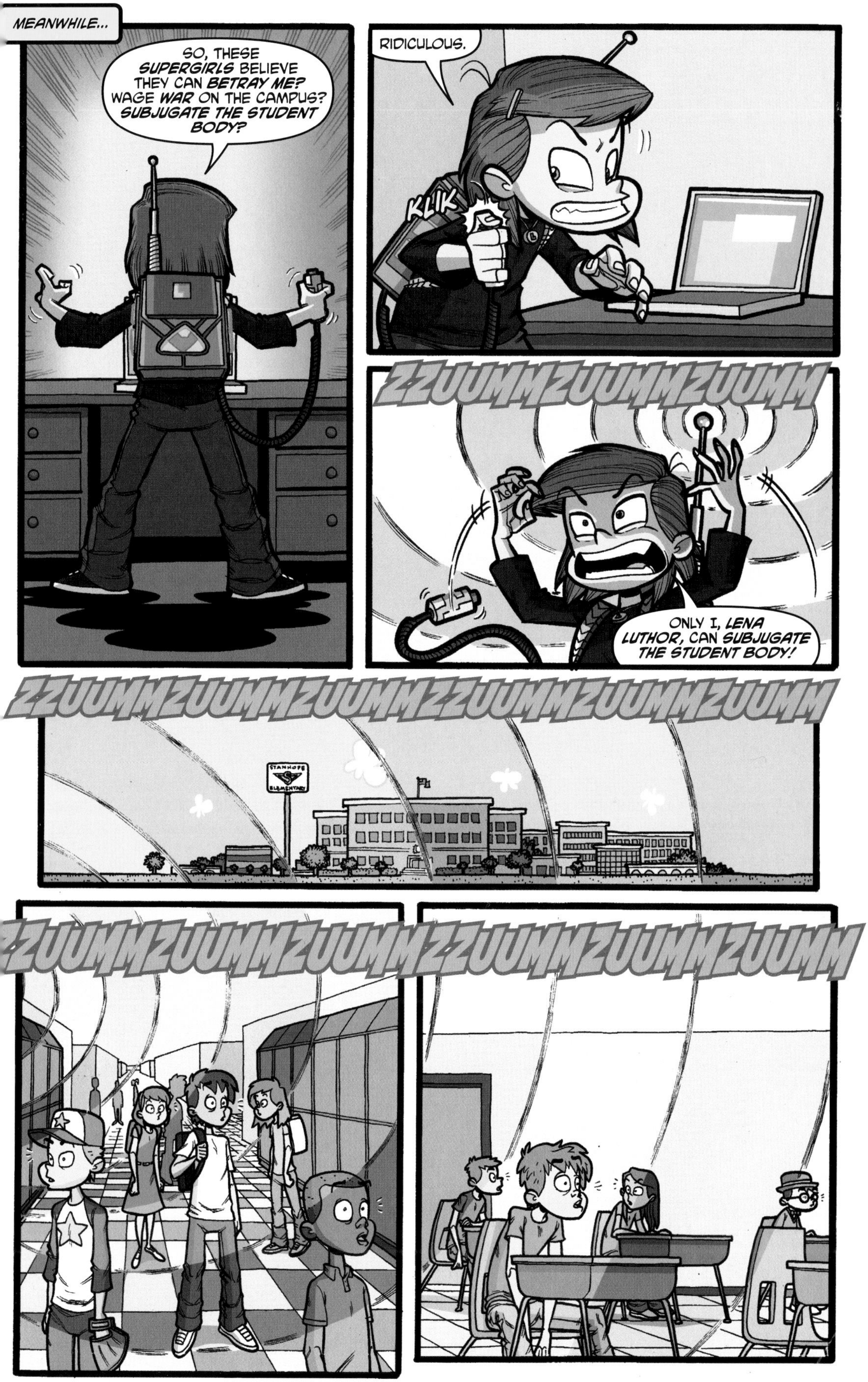

MEANWHILE...
SO, THESE SUPERGIRLS BELIEVE THEY CAN BETRAY ME? WAGE WAR ON THE CAMPUS? SUBJUGATE THE STUDENT BODY?
RIDICULOUS.
KLIK
ZZUUMMZUUMMZUUMM
ONLY I, LENA LUTHOR, CAN SUBJUGATE THE STUDENT BODY!
ZZUUMMZUUMMZUUMMZZUUMMZUUMMZUUMM
STANHOPE ELEMENTARY
ZZUUMMZUUMMZUUMMZZUUMMZUUMMZUUMM

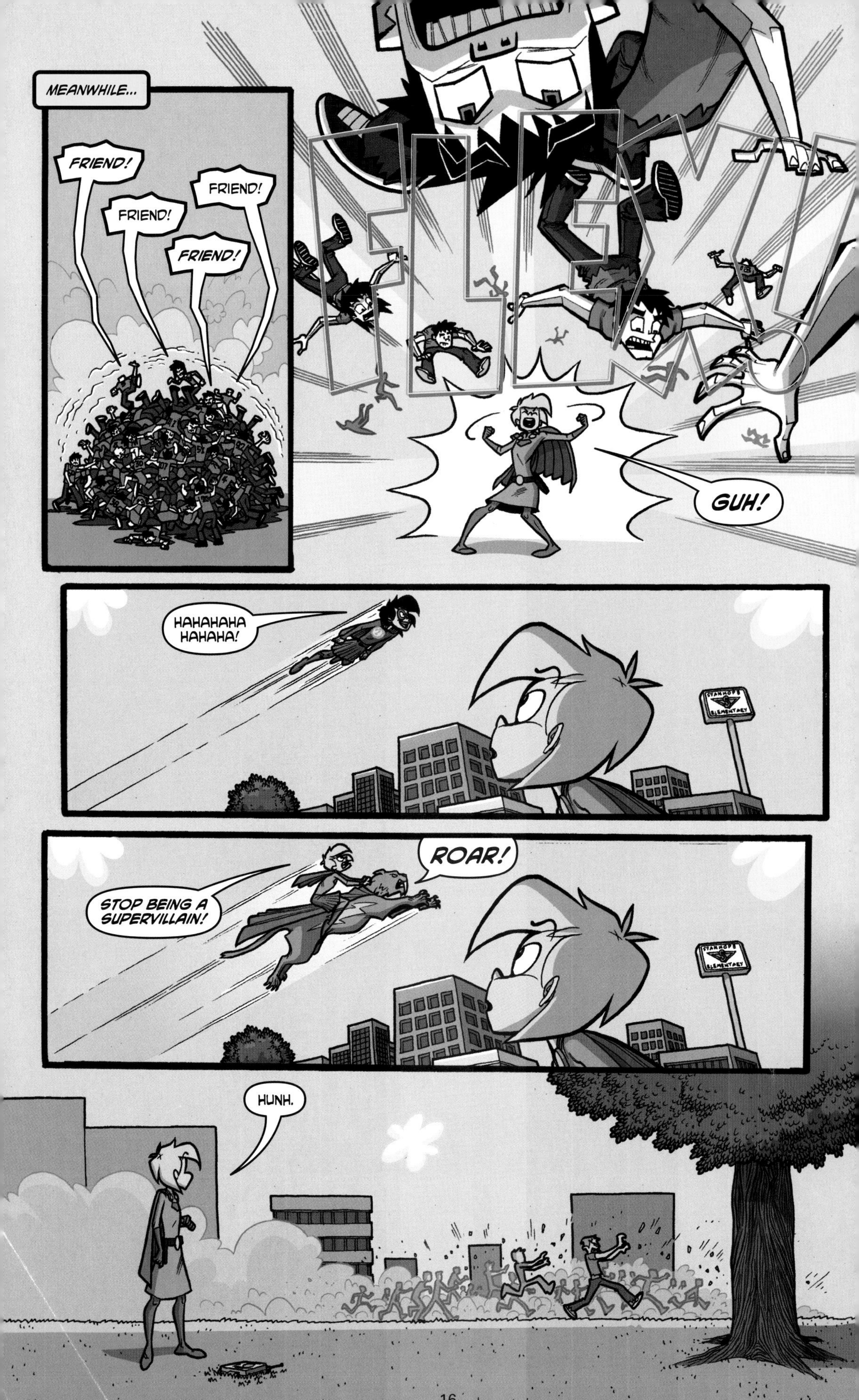
MEANWHILE...
FRIEND!
FRIEND!
FRIEND!
FRIEND!
GUH!
HAHAHAHA HAHAHA!
STOP BEING A SUPERVILLAIN!
ROAR!
HUNH.

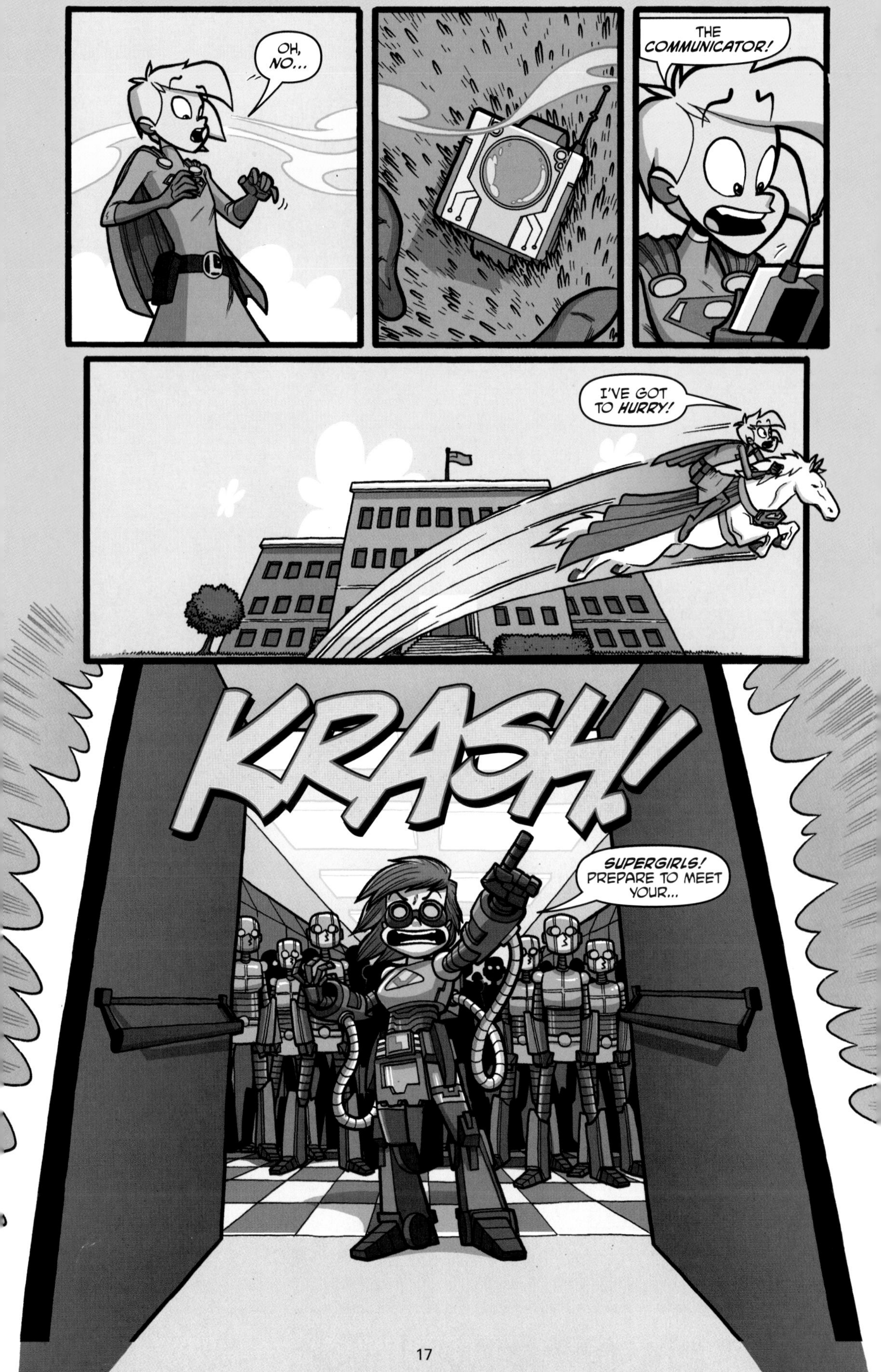
OH, NO...
THE COMMUNICATOR!
I'VE GOT TO HURRY!
KRASH!
SUPERGIRLS! PREPARE TO MEET YOUR...

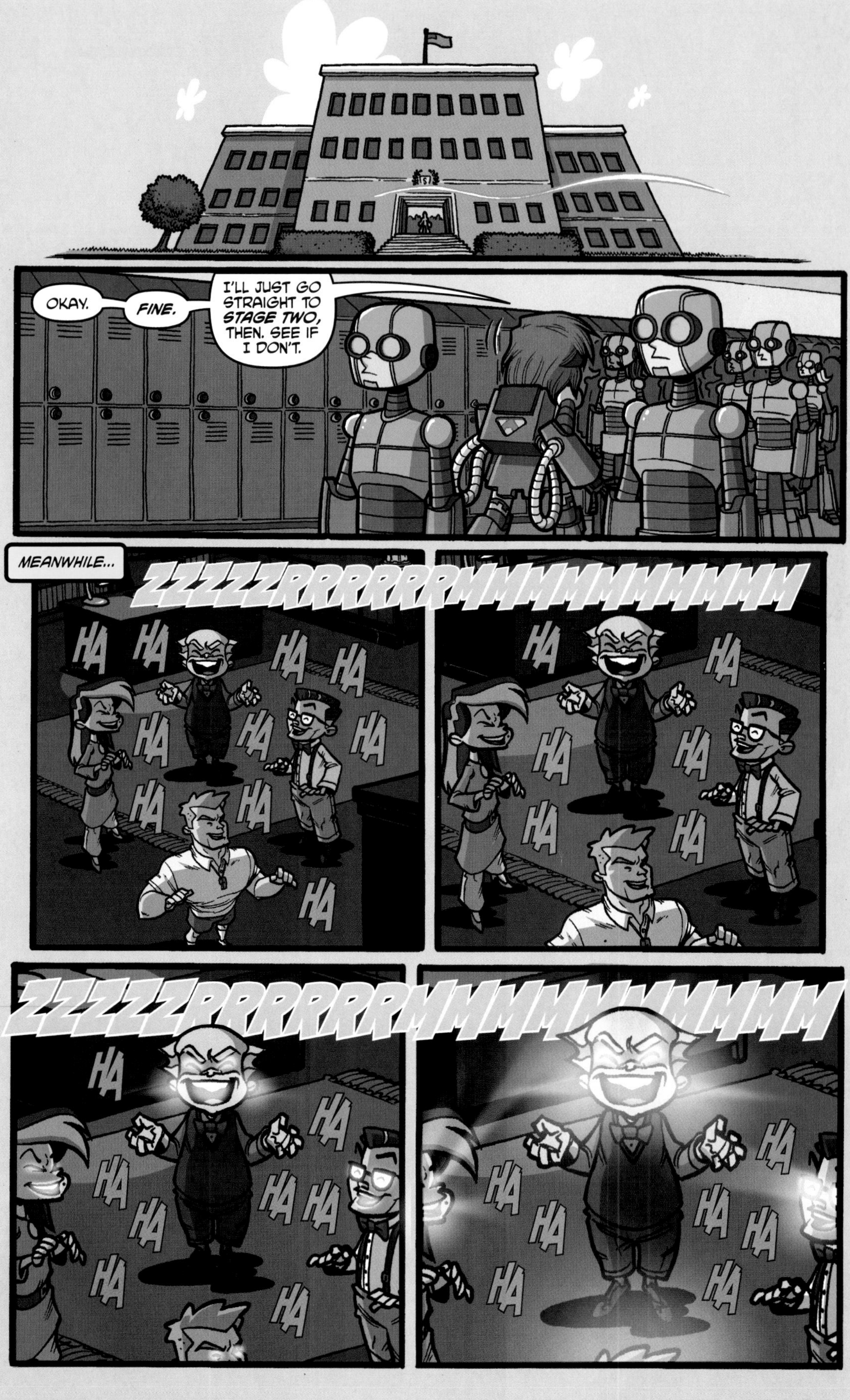
OKAY.
FINE.
I'LL JUST GO STRAIGHT TO STAGE TWO, THEN. SEE IF I DON'T.
MEANWHILE...
ZZZZZRRRRRRMMMMMMMMMMM
HA HA HA HA HA HA HA HA HA HA HA
HA HA HA HA HA HA HA
ZZZZZRRRRRRRMMMMMMMMMMMMM
HA HA HA HA HA HA HA HA HA
HA HA HA HA HA HA HA HA HA HA

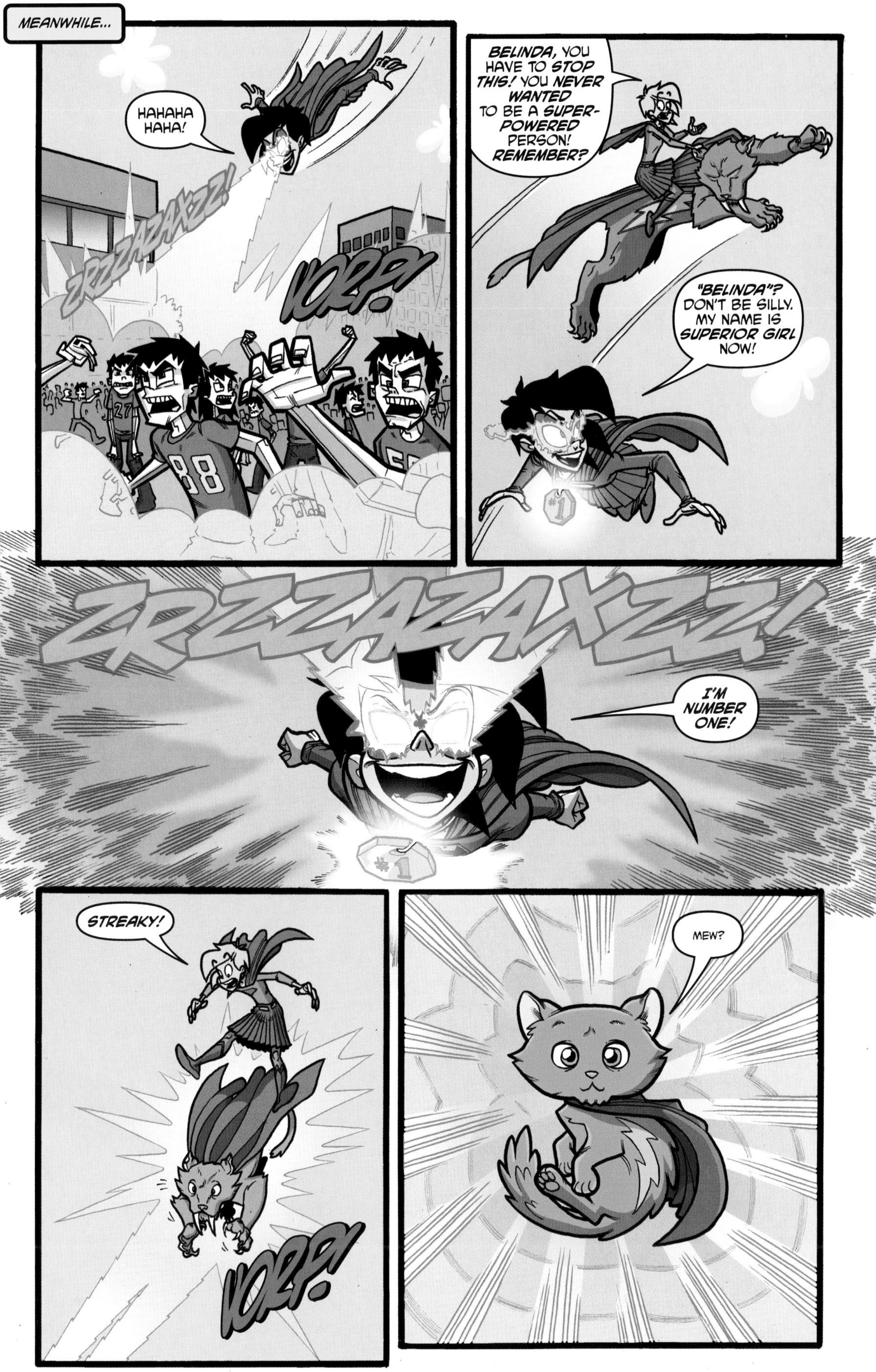
MEANWHILE...
HAHAHA HAHA!
ZRZZZAZAXZZ!
VORP!
BELINDA, YOU HAVE TO STOP THIS! YOU NEVER WANTED TO BE A SUPER-POWERED PERSON! REMEMBER?
"BELINDA"? DON'T BE SILLY. MY NAME IS SUPERIOR GIRL NOW!
ZRZZZAZAXZZ!
I'M NUMBER ONE!
STREAKY!
VORP!
MEW?

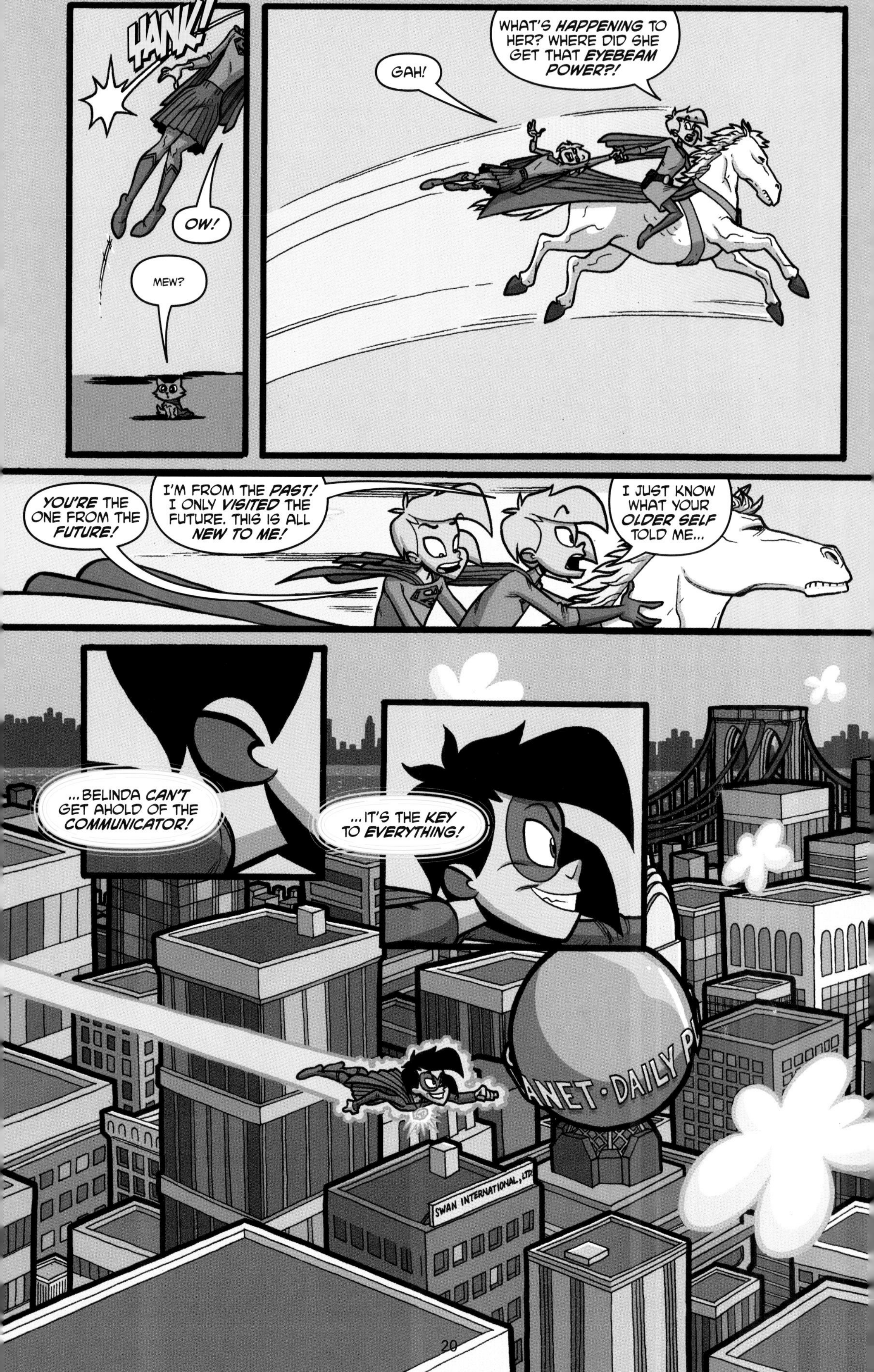

HANK!
OW!
MEW?
GAH!
WHAT'S HAPPENING TO HER? WHERE DID SHE GET THAT EYEBEAM POWER?!
YOU'RE THE ONE FROM THE FUTURE!
I'M FROM THE PAST! I ONLY VISITED THE FUTURE. THIS IS ALL NEW TO ME!
I JUST KNOW WHAT YOUR OLDER SELF TOLD ME...
...BELINDA CAN'T GET AHOLD OF THE COMMUNICATOR!
...IT'S THE KEY TO EVERYTHING!
ANET · DAILY P
SWAN INTERNATIONAL, LTD.

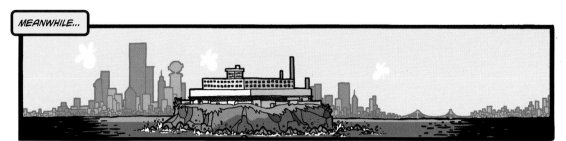

ALL RIGHT, *LUTHOR*. THE WARDEN FORWARDED YOUR *THREATS* TO ME, AND I ALREADY DEACTIVATED YOUR HIDDEN *ENTROPY BOMBS*. YOU SHOULD KNOW BETTER THAN TO PLAN AN *ESCAPE FROM PRISON* BY NOW.

"ESCAPE"? DO YOU REALLY THINK THAT I, *LEX LUTHOR*, COULD EVER BE *CONTAINED?* I RESIDE HERE OF *MY OWN VOLITION*, AND I WILL LEAVE AT A *TIME OF MY CHOOSING!*

I DON'T HAVE TIME FOR YOUR *GAMES*, LUTHOR...

AGH!

SZZXXXRAXX!

I JUST HAPPEN TO CHOOSE *NOW*, SUPER FOOL!

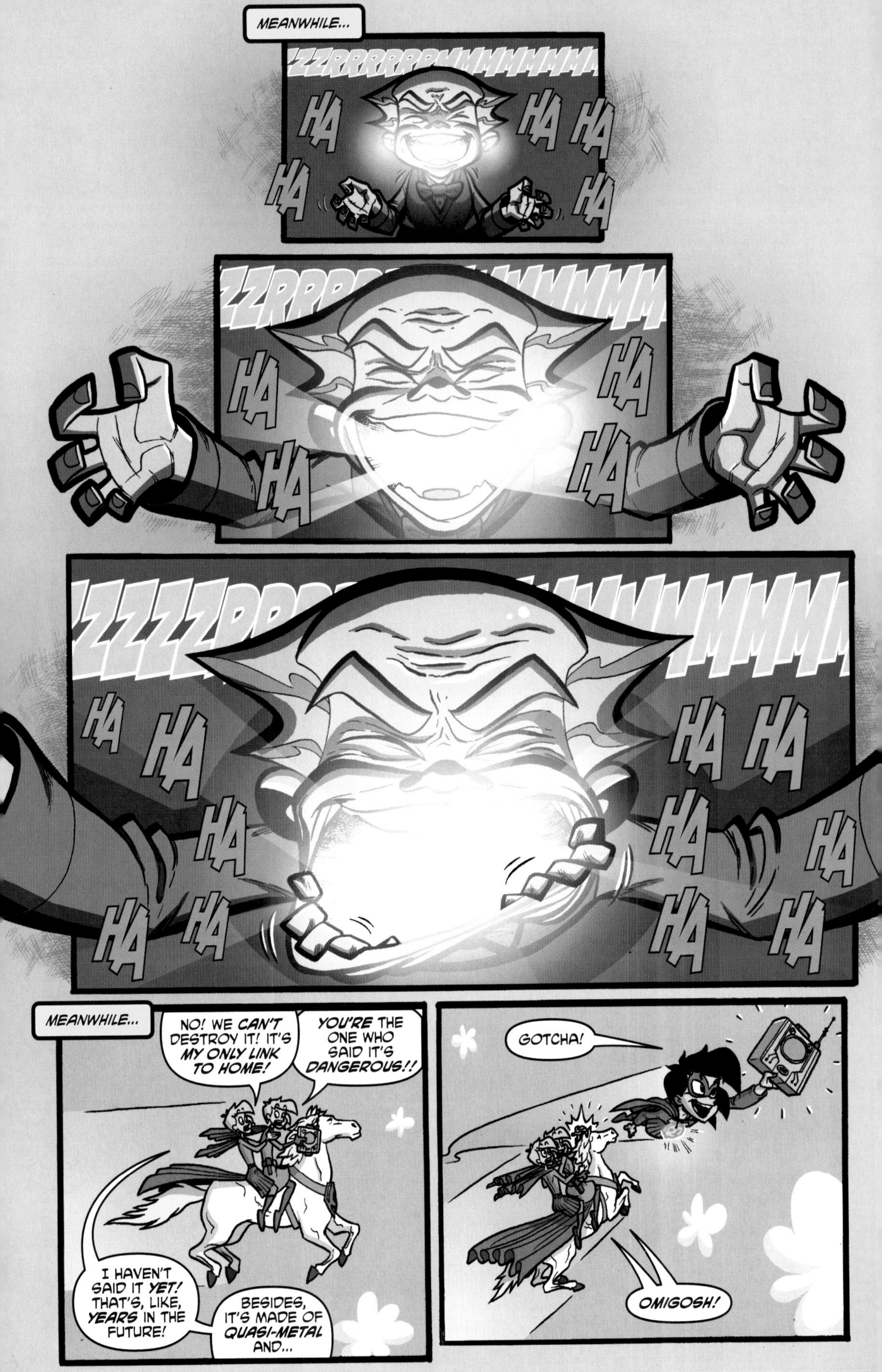

MEANWHILE...
ZZRRRRRRMMMMMMM
HA
HA
HA HA
HA
ZZRRRRMMMMMMM
HA
HA
HA
HA
ZZZZZRRRRMMMMMMMM
HA HA
HA
HA
HA
HA HA
HA
HA
HA HA
MEANWHILE...
NO! WE CAN'T DESTROY IT! IT'S MY ONLY LINK TO HOME!
YOU'RE THE ONE WHO SAID IT'S DANGEROUS!!
I HAVEN'T SAID IT YET! THAT'S, LIKE, YEARS IN THE FUTURE!
BESIDES, IT'S MADE OF QUASI-METAL AND...
GOTCHA!
OMIGOSH!

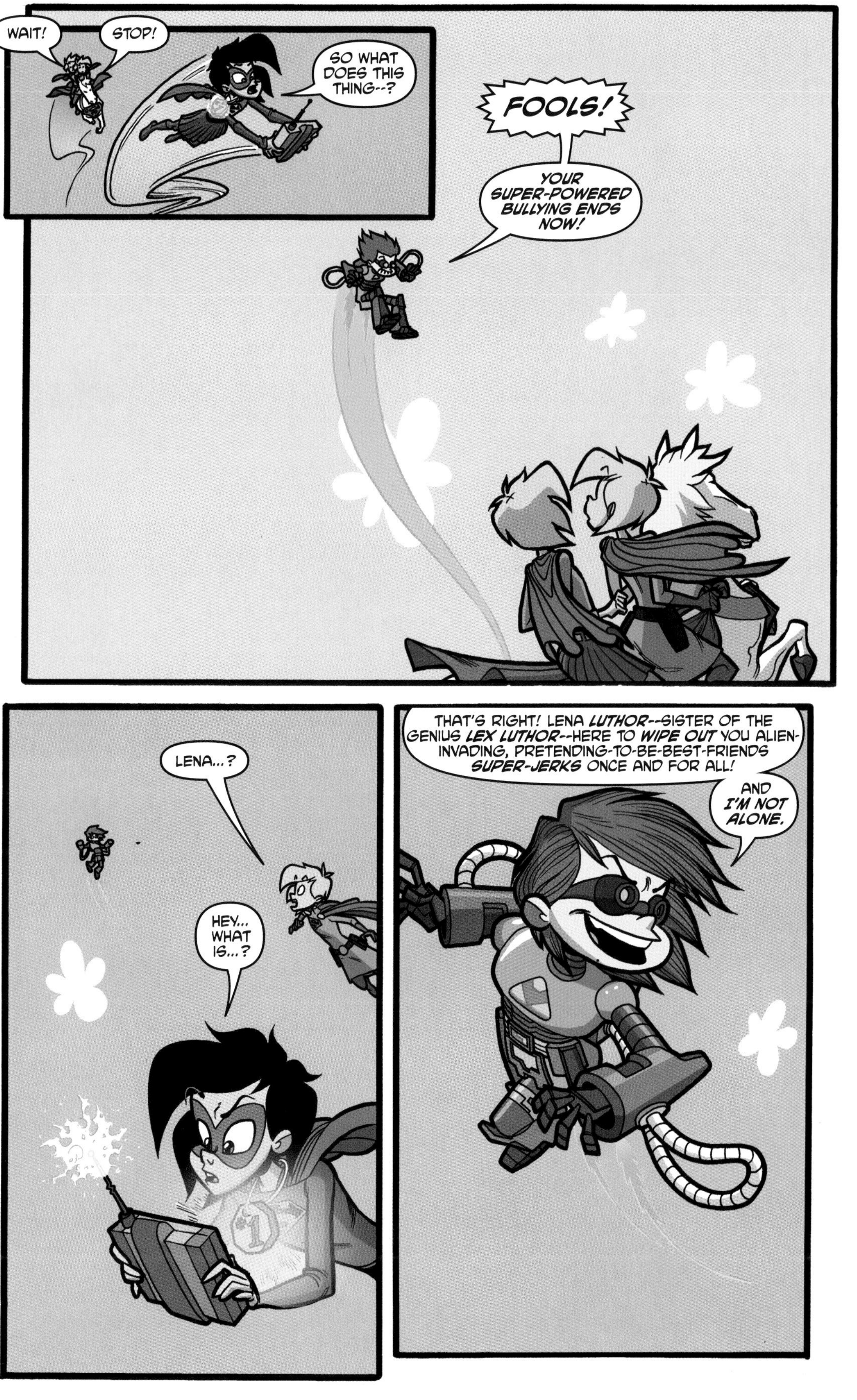
WAIT!
STOP!
SO WHAT DOES THIS THING--?
FOOLS!
YOUR SUPER-POWERED BULLYING ENDS NOW!
LENA...?
HEY... WHAT IS...?
THAT'S RIGHT! LENA LUTHOR--SISTER OF THE GENIUS LEX LUTHOR--HERE TO WIPE OUT YOU ALIEN-INVADING, PRETENDING-TO-BE-BEST-FRIENDS SUPER-JERKS ONCE AND FOR ALL!
AND I'M NOT ALONE.

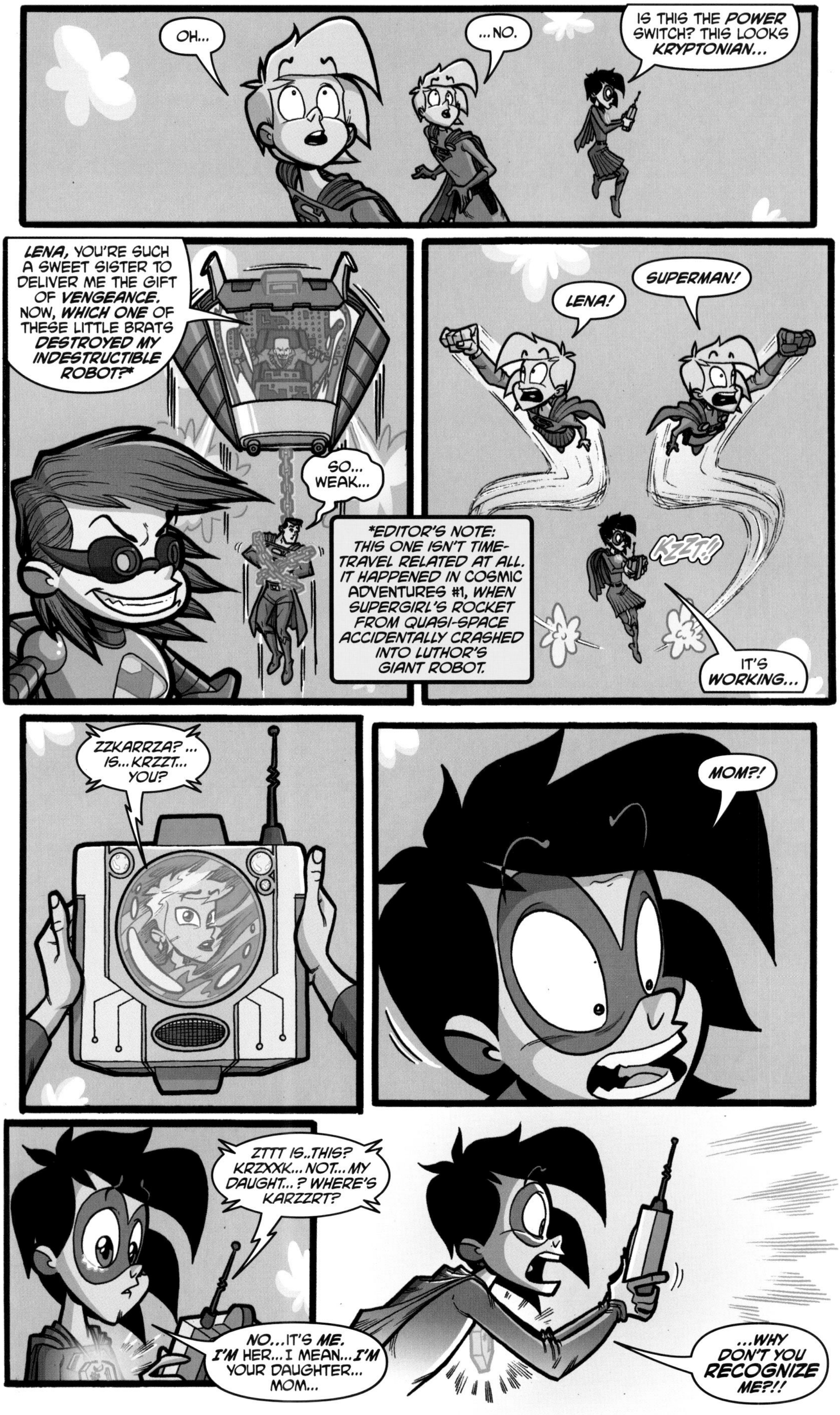
OH...
...NO.
IS THIS THE POWER SWITCH? THIS LOOKS KRYPTONIAN...
LENA, YOU'RE SUCH A SWEET SISTER TO DELIVER ME THE GIFT OF VENGEANCE. NOW, WHICH ONE OF THESE LITTLE BRATS DESTROYED MY INDESTRUCTIBLE ROBOT?*
SO... WEAK...
*EDITOR'S NOTE: THIS ONE ISN'T TIME-TRAVEL RELATED AT ALL. IT HAPPENED IN COSMIC ADVENTURES #1, WHEN SUPERGIRL'S ROCKET FROM QUASI-SPACE ACCIDENTALLY CRASHED INTO LUTHOR'S GIANT ROBOT.
LENA!
SUPERMAN!
KZZT!!
IT'S WORKING...
ZZKARRZA? ... IS...KRZZT... YOU?
MOM?!
ZTTT IS..THIS? KRZXXK... NOT... MY DAUGHT...? WHERE'S KARZZRT?
NO...IT'S ME. I'M HER...I MEAN...I'M YOUR DAUGHTER... MOM...
...WHY DON'T YOU RECOGNIZE ME?!!

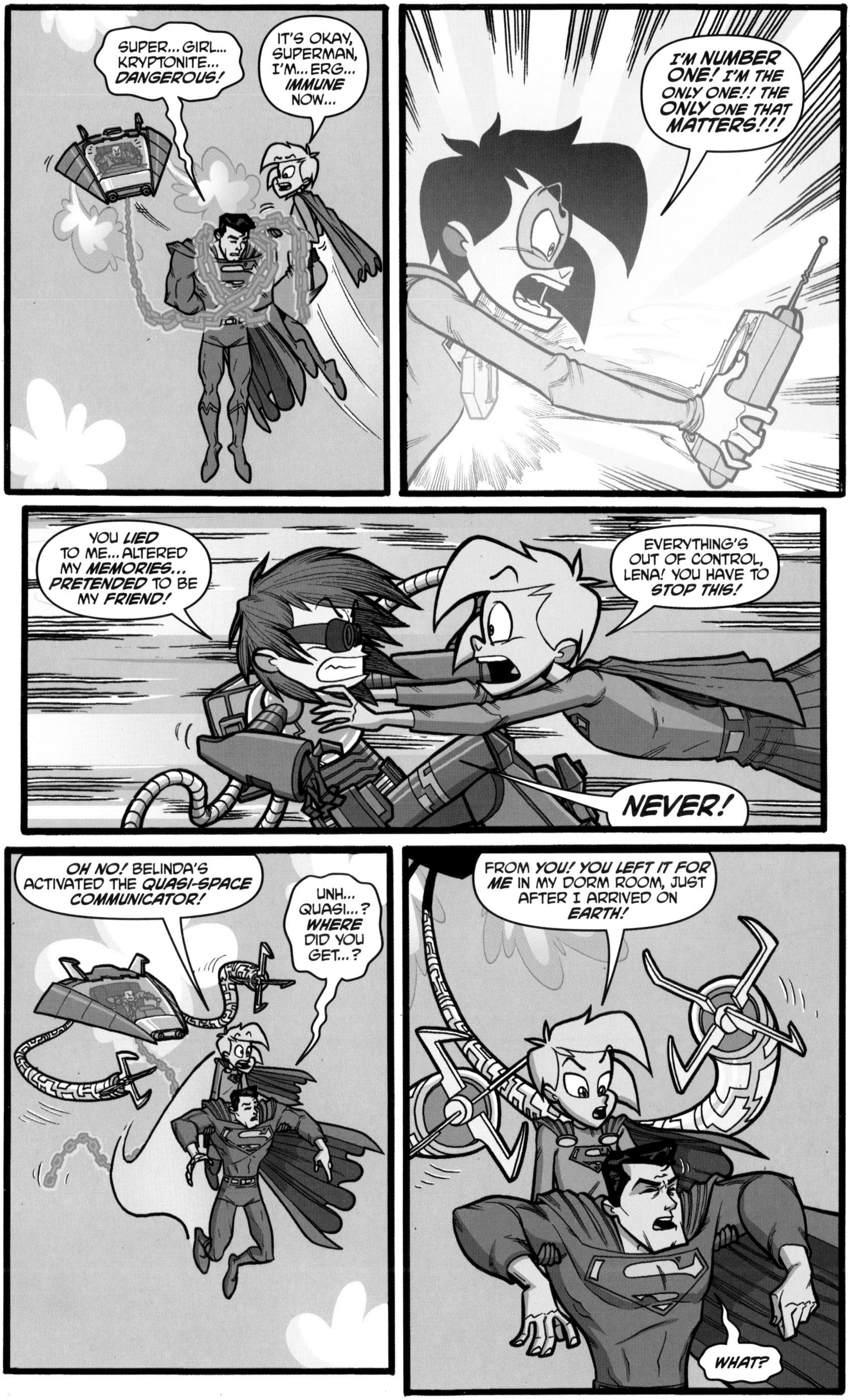
SUPER... GIRL... KRYPTONITE... DANGEROUS!
IT'S OKAY, SUPERMAN, I'M... ERG... IMMUNE NOW...
I'M NUMBER ONE! I'M THE ONLY ONE!! THE ONLY ONE THAT MATTERS!!!
YOU LIED TO ME... ALTERED MY MEMORIES... PRETENDED TO BE MY FRIEND!
EVERYTHING'S OUT OF CONTROL, LENA! YOU HAVE TO STOP THIS!
NEVER!
OH NO! BELINDA'S ACTIVATED THE QUASI-SPACE COMMUNICATOR!
UNH... QUASI...? WHERE DID YOU GET...?
FROM YOU! YOU LEFT IT FOR ME IN MY DORM ROOM, JUST AFTER I ARRIVED ON EARTH!
WHAT?

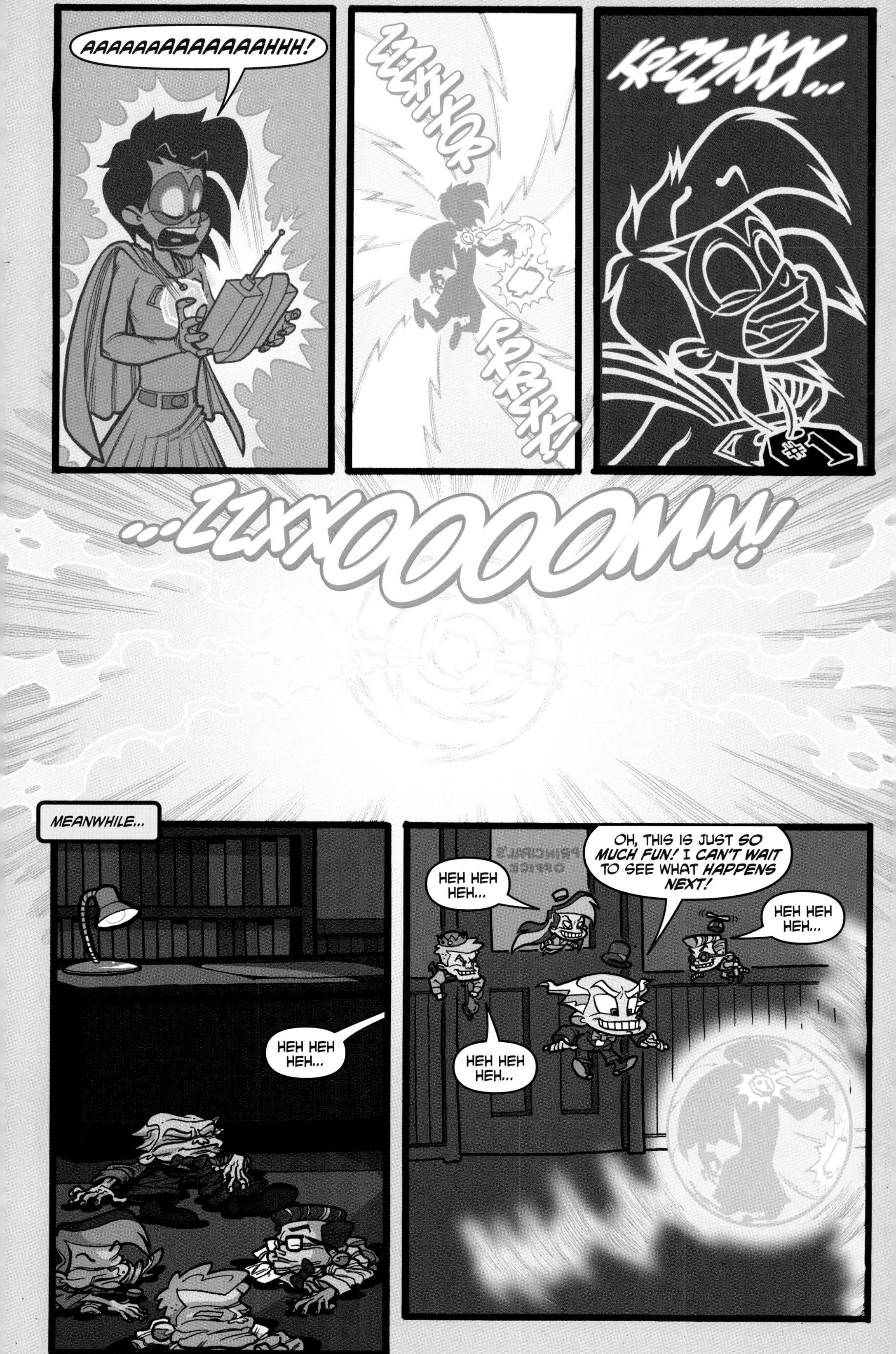

AAAAAAAAAAAAAAHHH!
ZZZXXXOR
RRRRKK!
KRZZZXXX...
...ZZXXOOOOOMM!
MEANWHILE...
HEH HEH HEH...
PRINCIPAL'S OFFICE
HEH HEH HEH...
OH, THIS IS JUST SO MUCH FUN! I CAN'T WAIT TO SEE WHAT HAPPENS NEXT!
HEH HEH HEH...
HEH HEH HEH...

CREATORS

LANDRY Q. WALKER WRITER

Landry Q. Walker is a comics writer whose projects include *Supergirl: Cosmic Adventures in the 8th Grade* and more. He has also written *Batman: The Brave and the Bold,* the comic book adventures of The Incredibles, and contributed stories to *Disney Adventures* magazine and the gaming website Elder-Geek.

ERIC JONES ARTIST

Eric Jones is a professional comic book artist whose work for DC Comics include *Batman: The Brave and the Bold, Supergirl: Cosmic Adventures in the 8th Grade, Cartoon Network Action Pack,* and more.

JOEY MASON COLORIST

Joey Mason is an illustrator, animation artist, and comic book colorist. His work for DC Comics includes *Supergirl: Cosmic Adventures in the 8th Grade,* as well as set designs for *Green Lantern: The Animated Series.*

GLOSSARY

arrogant [A·ruh·guhnt]-conceited and too proud
degradation [deg·ruh·DAY·shuhn]-a loss of honor or reputation
entropy [EN·truh·pee]-the degree of disorder or uncertainty in a system
immune [i·MYOON]-protected against a certain disease or potentially harmful substance
invulnerability [in·vuhl·nur·uh·BILL·i·tee]-immunity to harm
miserable [MIZ·ur·uh·buhl]-sad, unhappy, or dejected
paradox [PA·ruh·doks]-a person or thing that seems to contradict itself
refugee [ref·yuh·JEE]-a person who is forced to leave his or her home because of war, persecution, or natural disaster
spite [SPITE]-to be mean or nasty to
subjugate [SUB·juh·gate]-to bring under control or make submissive
succumb [suh·KUM]-give in to superior strength, force, or influence
vortex [VORE·teks]-something that resembles a whirlpool

VISUAL QUESTIONS & PROMPTS

1. Based on what you've read in this comic book, who do you think this character with the purple hat is? What are his powers? Why is he influencing Supergirl's life?

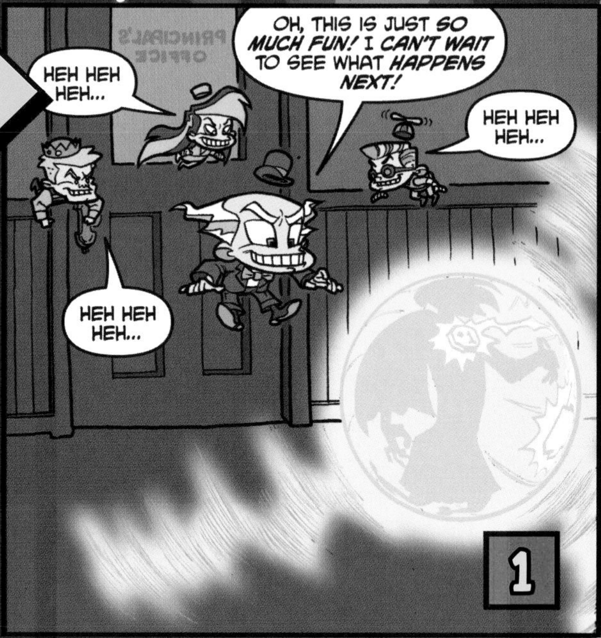
PRINCIPAL'S OFFICE
HEH HEH HEH...
OH, THIS IS JUST SO MUCH FUN! I CAN'T WAIT TO SEE WHAT HAPPENS NEXT!
HEH HEH HEH...
HEH HEH HEH...
1

2. Sometimes sound effects, or SFX, aren't actually sounds. What are some other sound-related words that could replace "FLEX!" in the panel below? Get creative!

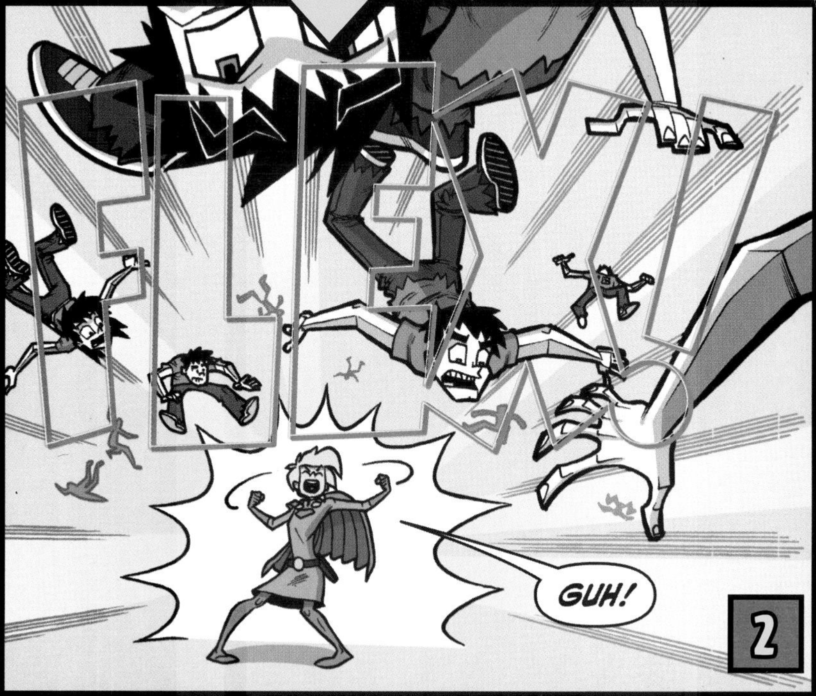
FLEX!
GUH!
2

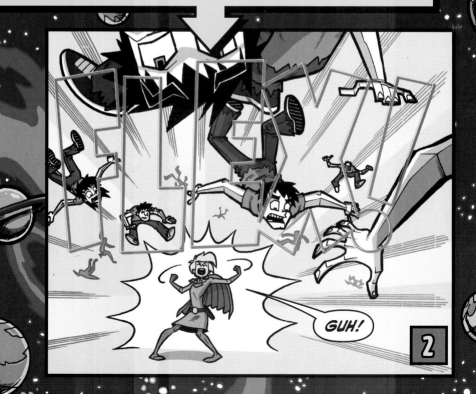

3. Read the glossary definition of "invulnerability" then explain what Supergirl means when she thanks her invulnerability in this panel.

THANK YOU, INVULNERABILITY. YOU ARE MY VERY BESTEST FRIEND...
3

4
ECAUSE I'M ON BACK IN TIME IT FROM EVER PENING!**
BUT... WHY ARE YOU HERE?
**EDITOR'S NOTE: SHE IS, AND SHE DID. AGAIN, IN COSMIC ADVENTURES #3.
I DON'T REALLY KNOW. ALL I KNOW IS WHAT YOU TOLD ME...
WHAT? I DIDN'T...
OH... YOU DON'T TELL ME ABOUT IT UNTIL WE MEET IN THE 30TH CENTURY. THAT'S WHEN I GOT THIS COOL BELT!***
***EDITOR'S NOTE: THIS HAS NOT ACTUALLY HAPPENED. YET.
RIGHT. AND IS THAT WHERE YOU GOT THE HORSE?
COMET? OH YEAH, HE BELONGS TO YOU IN THE FUTURE. YOU LOANED HIM TO ME.****
****EDITOR'S NOTE: OKAY, ENOUGH OF THIS. IT'S TIME TRAVEL. YOU GET THE IDEA.

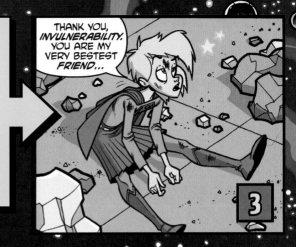

4. The yellow boxes that appear throughout this book are called "editor's notes." Most comics don't have many of these boxes, but this one does. Why were they necessary to include in this book?

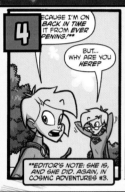

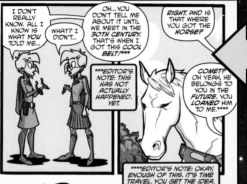

5. In your own words, explain why the illustrator chose to include lines behing little-kitty-Streaky in the second panel.

STREAKY!
VORP!
MEW?
5

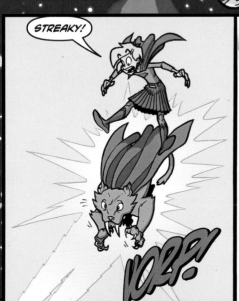

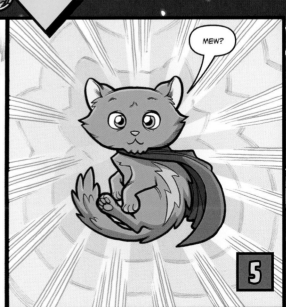

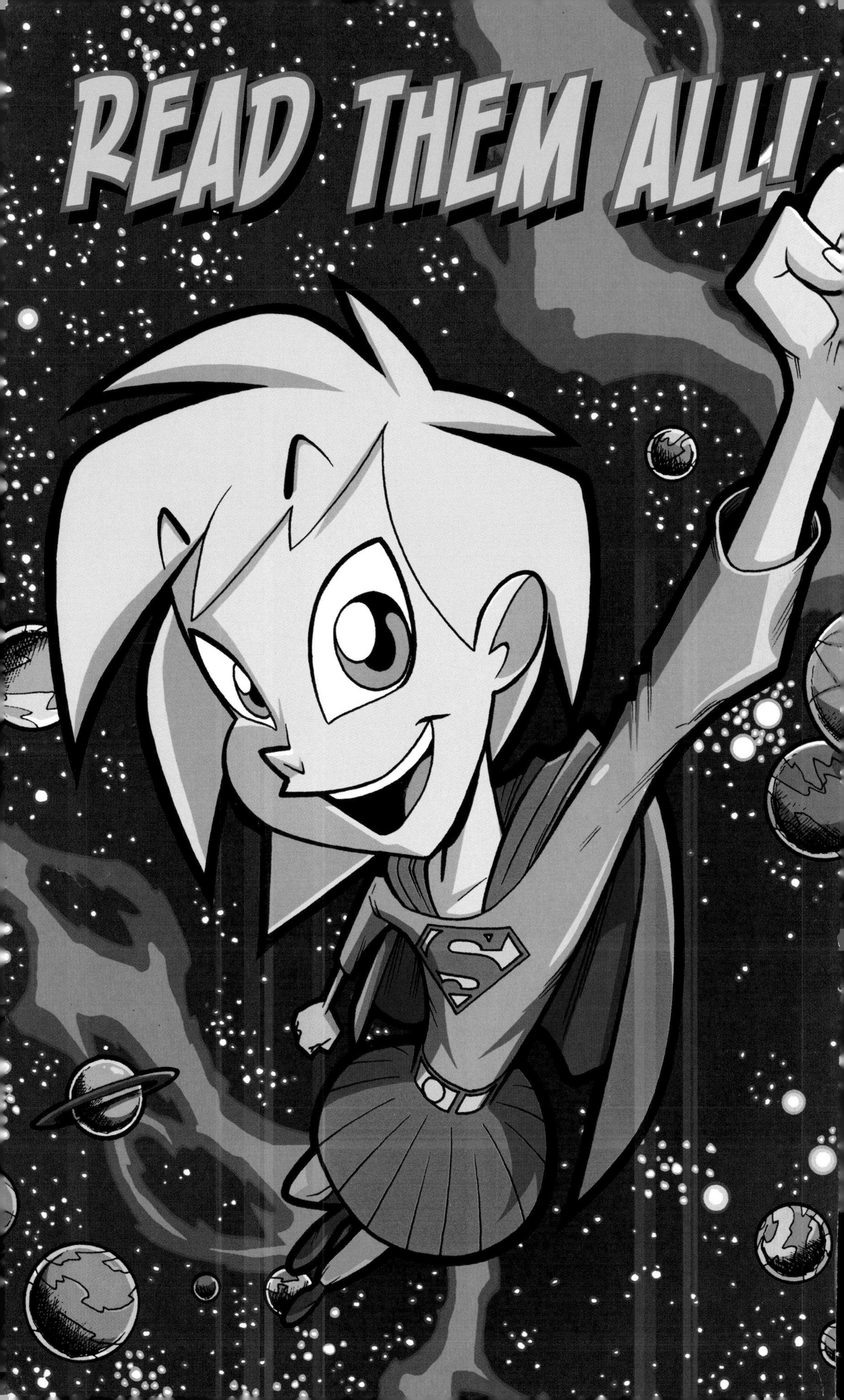
READ THEM ALL!

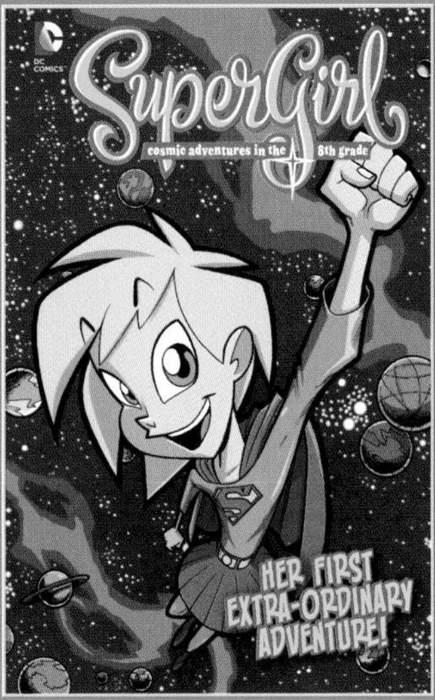
DC COMICS
SuperGirl
cosmic adventures in the 8th grade
HER FIRST EXTRA-ORDINARY ADVENTURE!

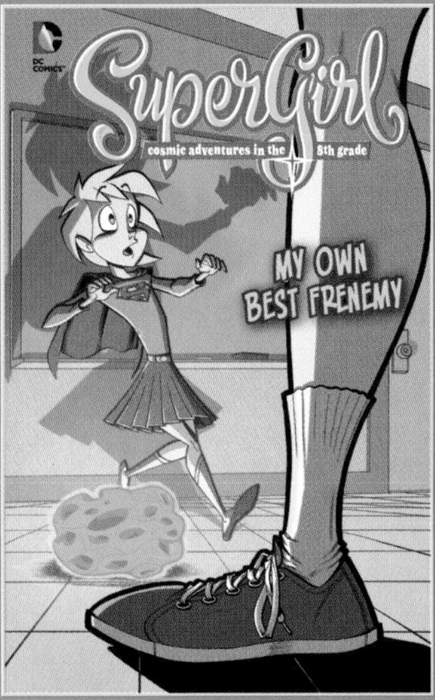
DC COMICS
SuperGirl
cosmic adventures in the 8th grade
MY OWN BEST FRENEMY

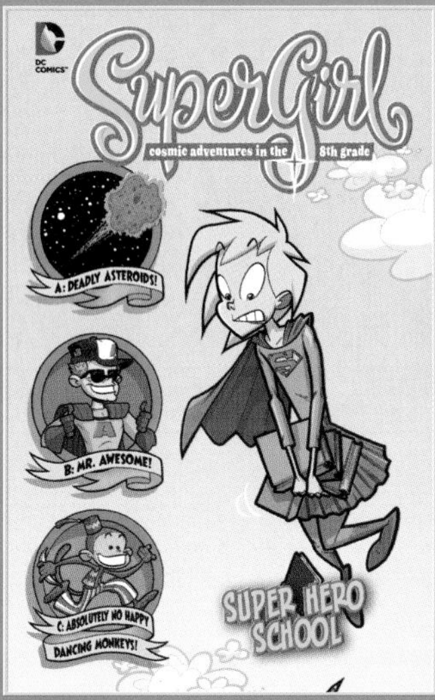
DC COMICS
SuperGirl
cosmic adventures in the 8th grade
A: DEADLY ASTEROIDS!
B: MR. AWESOME!
C: ABSOLUTELY NO HAPPY DANCING MONKEYS!
SUPER HERO SCHOOL

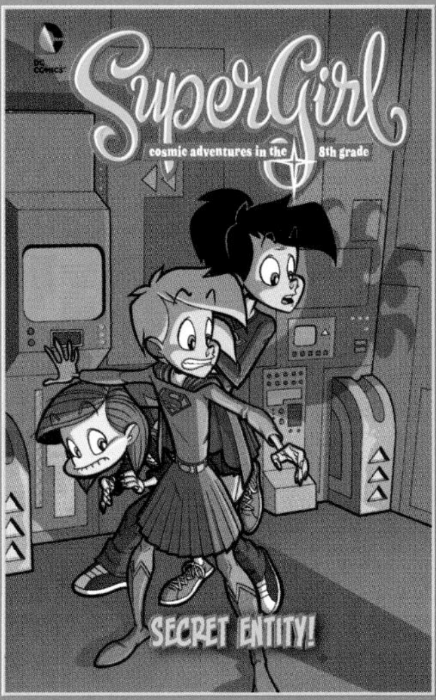
DC COMICS
SuperGirl
cosmic adventures in the 8th grade
SECRET ENTITY!

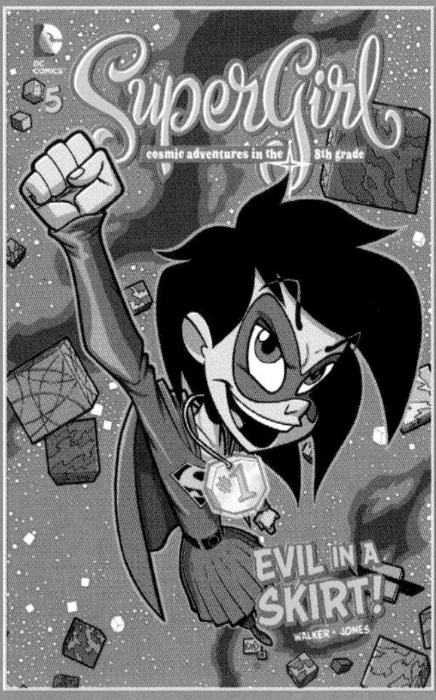
DC COMICS
5
SuperGirl
cosmic adventures in the 8th grade
#1
EVIL IN A SKIRT!
WALKER · JONES

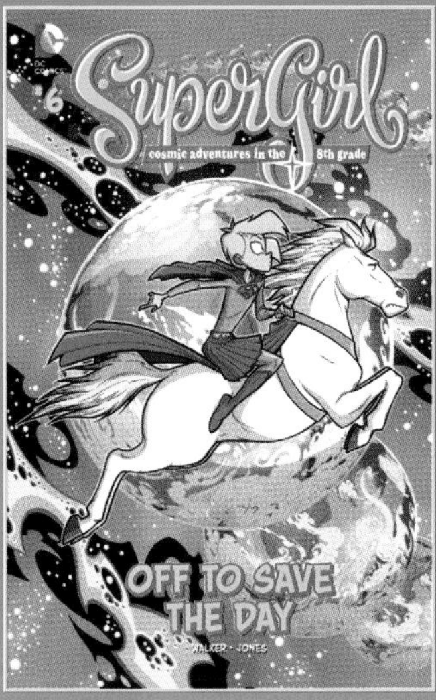
DC COMICS
6
SuperGirl
cosmic adventures in the 8th grade
OFF TO SAVE THE DAY
WALKER · JONES

ONLY FROM...

STONE ARCH BOOKS™

a capstone imprint www.capstonepub.com

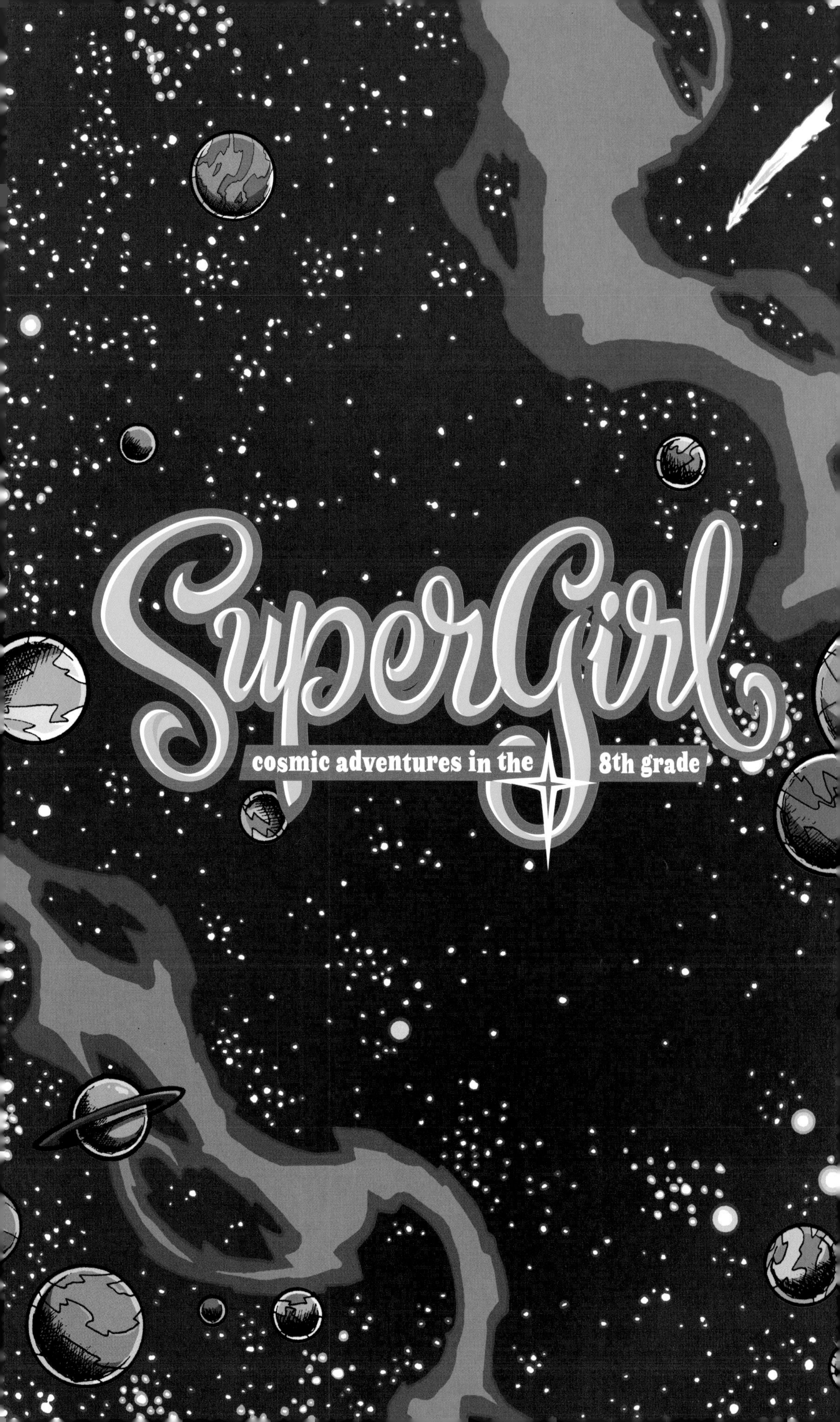
SuperGirl
cosmic adventures in the 8th grade